W9-AUJ-028

LOSS ANGELES

STORIES

MATHIEU CAILLER

ISBN: 978-0-9882497-4-5
Library of Congress Control Number: 2015931061

Printed in the United States of America

Jacket photo by Chaz Cipolla
Author photo by James Ferrari

Publisher: Short Story America Press
Design: Soundview Design Studio

Short Story America
221 Johnson Landing Road
Beaufort, SC 29907
Visit us online at www.shortstoryamerica.com

Pour Maman et Papa—

toujours nous trois

The author wishes to thank the following publications where these stories first appeared, some in slightly different form: "Over the Bridge," "Dark Timber," and "One-Night Stand" in *Short Story America Volume III*; "A Day Like Today" in *Pithead Chapel*; "Dissonance" in *Epiphany*; "Graveyard Shift" in *The Ofi Press, Mexico*; "Birds of Paradise" in *The Santa Fe Literary Review*; "Hit and Stay" in *Two Hawks Quarterly*; "Do You See the Big Dipper?" in *Daily Love*; "Neighbors" in *Riprap Literary Journal*; "Zorba's" in *Scissors and Spackle*; "Blowing Out the Candles" in *Sleet Magazine*; "When Men Wore Hats" in *Ardor Literary Magazine*.

CONTENTS

OVER THE BRIDGE

* * *

It was another one o'clock on another Friday, and there I sat in Mrs. Zohorian's office for our weekly meeting. Ever since Mom died, the school thought it would help me to "talk things out," but I knew it helped them too, maybe more than it was supposed to help me.

Mrs. Z was an Alaska of a woman—gigantic thighs, multiple chins, and sausage-like fingers. She sat on her padded office chair and asked question after question in a soft voice: "Ella, you feeling better this week?"

"About the same," I said.

Mrs. Z scribbled something on her notepad. I scanned her office. Inspirational posters lined the walls—a picture of a girl running up stairs with the word "Perseverance" across the top, two kids in polo shirts playing chess with "Strategy" hanging above them, and spring flowers blossoming with "Resilience" in all capitals. I wondered where Mrs. Z bought these posters. Was there a store for high school counselors?

"What class did I pull you out of?" Mrs. Z popped in a mint to battle her breath. Altoids couldn't handle her stuff, though.

"Math."

"What were you studying?"

"Stuff on triangles—the Pythagorean Theorem and Soh Cah Toa."

"Soh Cah what?"

"It's just this way of remembering what to do for sine and cosine."

Sometimes Mrs. Z hoped that generic questions would lead to specific answers. I knew her strategy.

"How are things with your dad?" she said.

"About the same. It's just strange living with him again, you know? My brother and I were used to seeing him every other weekend, but now it's every day. We were used to Mom's house, and Dad's place is loud."

"Have you talked to him about this?"

"Not really. Mostly he does his thing and I do mine."

"You really need to talk to him, Ella. I was thinking," Mrs. Z said, clicking her pen, "why don't you write him a letter? Not to give to him or anything, but just to get it out. Writing can be cathartic. When my father died in college, I wrote him letters from time to time. Here, take this." She yanked a blank piece of paper from her printer and found a school envelope in her desk drawer.

I rolled my office chair to a nearby table. Mrs. Z jotted more things down on her pad and then typed something into Google.

Trying to make Mrs. Z happy, I wrote *Dad* on the front of the envelope in my largest, loopiest cursive. I even underlined the word a few times.

This was one of those assignments, I thought, where the teacher or counselor grabbed a break on the job. It was smart, like the responsible, adult version of doodling. She totally believed that she was doing something by having me write a letter. Meanwhile, she was browsing at Zappos.

A bowl of half-eaten noodles sat next to Mrs. Z's mouse pad, reminding me of Mom's last night: She doesn't want to cook during the week, but that night she says she feels like it. She picks out a CD, Bob Dylan's *Freewheelin'*. I tell her I like the cover—a man huddled with a woman, walking a powdery New York street. Mom has Johnny practice his reading by having him read the recipe aloud. Johnny says *miced* instead of *minced,* and Mom corrects him. He laughs. After we drop in the ground beef, onions, garlic, salt, pepper, and one egg, we pile our hands into the bowl and mix it into meatballs. Six hands, one bowl.

Knowing that time would move faster if I just started Mrs. Z's assignment, I got to work. *Dear Dad,* I wrote, *It's been almost three months since the accident and more than four years since your guys' divorce.* I thought about the apostrophe after "guys." It didn't look right, then it did, then it didn't again. There wasn't a Soh Cah Toa for apostrophes. *It's been a long time since we've lived together… sure, we had every other weekend, but I mean really lived together. It's also been a long time since we've been close. I don't know what happened. One day it was hard to talk to you, the next day the same, but here we are. I'd like us to be close… like when I was little, really little. I guess when I had Mom I didn't think about it as much, but now I really need you. Johnny really needs you. Can you imagine not having your mom at seven? We don't just need you to ask how school was or sign permission slips like you do. Do you even love us? I know Mom loved us, but do you? How'd you feel about Mom dying? You didn't cry at the funeral. You didn't hug us. You just stood there in your black suit. How do you feel about anything? I guess I just want to talk to you, and I hope that you want to talk to me.* I looked around. My gaze bumped into Mrs. Z's.

"Everything all right?" she said, looking at her watch. She'd scrolled through the pumps and was honing in on a pair of red flats.

"Yeah."

"All right, Ella," Mrs. Z said, just as I signed my name. "That's it for today. Because of the assembly this morning our session was shortened. We'll get back to it next week. Oh, one more thing. I got a new cell phone number, so let me give it to you. Actually, let me just put my number directly into your phone." Before I knew it, she'd rolled her chair over to me, and her fat fingers were pecking at my phone. "Have a beautiful weekend, Ella. Be safe."

I closed my eyes and nodded. With a quick swipe of my tongue, I sealed the letter and shoved it into my back pocket.

I returned to math class and took my seat behind Bridgette. Bridgette was the perfect tenth grader—her hair, shiny and wavy, her body, lean and airbrushed. She'd received a puberty pass—no acne, no growth spurt, no in-transition breasts; it seemed as though she'd gotten all the hard, growing-up work out of the way while on summer vacation in Spain.

Mr. Nguyen, the math teacher, turned on the overhead projector and switched off the lights. I closed my eyes: Mom, grading papers at the kitchen table. One of her rings bothers her while she writes, so she drops it down the tail of the pewter cat ring holder. I stare at her bumpy knuckles and her pearl-colored nails. She hums a song. When I ask her what it is, she says it's a Miles Davis tune. "All Blues" it's called. Do-Doo, Do-Doo, Johnny puffs out his cheeks, sticks his thumb near his mouth and pretends to play.

Mr. Nguyen assigned four "real world" problems, my least favorite. They tried to show the connection between life and mathematics, just in case I ever needed to build a drawbridge or a gazebo. Basically, "real world" problems gave me the same headache as normal math problems, but with more reading.

Susie smiled at me from across the class. Only another twenty minutes and it'd be the weekend, time for Dylan's party. Mr. Nguyen popped his knuckles and cleared his throat. We got back to work.

* * *

After school, Susie drove me home. She'd been my friend since I was seven, so things were comfortable. Mom used to say that we'd accrued tenure by knowing one another for so long.

Susie was a year older than me and drove a crappy green Pontiac, a recent purchase from her summer job at In-N-Out Burger. She rolled down both front windows and slid in a CD of her cousin's punk band, Lost in the Crawlspace. The music was loud and angry and bashed my ears.

Our conversation revolved around Dylan's party and Brandon Sweets (Susie's kind-of boyfriend, whose last name wasn't really Sweets; it was something Polish that neither of us could pronounce, but we called him Sweets because he practically lived at the vending machine, always buying Grandma's Cookies or Starburst).

"Brandon's bringing a friend, too," Susie said, driving with her left hand as her right hand played with the radio.

"Is he cute?"

"I don't know! I didn't ask! It would've been weird. Plus guys never know if other guys are cute. And if they do, they never say." Susie laughed a little.

At my home, Susie texted Brandon while I changed clothes. I wanted to find something that would make me look great, but not something that would make me look like I was *trying* to look great, like going to Dylan's wasn't a big deal, even though I'd never been to his house.

"Why don't you wear that cute chiffon top with tights or

something?" Susie was good at being a girl. She knew hair and makeup and always called shirts "tops." I liked to wear sweatshirts that hung over my body and didn't expose my shape, or lack thereof. Mom's Mount Holyoke sweatshirt or Long Beach Faculty hoodie were best for that.

I put on the outfit that Susie had picked and rammed my jeans and sweatshirt into the hamper—it was bursting with clothes, mostly Johnny's grass-stained pants, and some of Dad's shirts that were strong with cigarette smoke.

"You look perfect," Susie said. "All you need now is a little makeup."

I sat on the floor while Susie hovered around me like an SAT proctor, inspecting me from all angles. "I can't decide what color eye shadow to go with," she said. "Something to make the flowers on your shirt pop; something Brandon's friend won't be able to handle! Your Dad knows that you're spending the night at my house tonight, right?"

"Yeah," I said.

"Good." Susie applied the brush to my eyelids.

After Susie fixed me up, I opened Mom's jewelry box and tried to pick out something that went with my outfit. So much for not trying too hard, I thought. This was the first time I was going to wear one of Mom's pieces. Most of the time, I just opened the box for a whiff of perfume.

I picked up a bracelet: Mom, making sure Johnny brushes his teeth. She tucks him in and goes through the how-far-open-do-you-want-me-to-leave-the-door routine. She comes by my room and stands in the doorframe. She's just painted her toenails, so she walks carefully. "Love you," she says, and waves goodnight with her fingers, not her wrist.

"What about this?" Susie said, holding up a necklace with a raindrop-shaped pendant.

I nodded and Susie brought the chain around my neck and fastened the latch. The metal was cold, but even cold, it made me feel close to Mom.

"How are you doing with it all?" Susie asked. "I feel like you're doing better."

"Yeah," I said.

I thought that if I answered that question that way enough times, I'd start to believe it. But sometimes I worried. If I lost my grief, I'd lose Mom. Last week, Mrs. Z told me that I'd learn how to live with hurt. She even went as far as to pick up my backpack. "See, to me," she said, grunting, "this is really heavy, but not for you, right? You know why? Because you're used to it. Trust me, Ella. You'll get stronger. Your family will get stronger. A day at a time." I was tired of people saying that it was just going to take time. Mom's accident wasn't a bad haircut.

"Good," Susie said. "You know if you need me…"

"Yeah," I said.

Sometimes I wanted to tell Susie how I really felt—that all I could think about was Mom, and how I missed eating eggs with her each morning while we laughed at our horoscopes. How I even missed looking for her car keys and reading glasses. All I wondered was why this had happened, and if I'd ever get better. Would I ever be that close to anyone again? Sometimes I thought about the stars, how Mom liked them so much. We'd drive away from the city, away from the lights. "Let your eyes get used to the dark," she'd say.

I walked to the bathroom, flipped open my phone, and read a text that Mom had sent me a while back. *Love you, el… good luck on your english test… you'll do great☺.*

The front door opened. "Ella?" Dad said.

"Ella!" Johnny said.

Susie told them I was in the bathroom. When I came out, Dad was polishing his saxophone. A cigarette dangled from his mouth and bits of ash fluttered to the floor. Johnny ran over and hugged me.

"How was school?" Dad asked.

"Good," I said. "You have a gig tonight?"

"Just a small one," he said. "Playing at a restaurant in Redondo. Should end early, though."

"What about Johnny?"

"He's coming with me."

"Is that a good idea?"

"Don't have much of a choice. You're gone for the night. It's fine… he'll just hang out."

Johnny went to the refrigerator, pulled out a slice of leftover pizza and warmed it in the microwave. "Don't stand so close," I told him. Since Mom had passed, I found myself using her words.

"So school was good?" Dad said.

"Yeah," I said.

"For you too, Susie?"

"Yup," she said.

"Good."

I studied him as he polished the sax's bell. There were black semicircles under his eyes. He hadn't shaved in a few days, and the stubble on his Adam's apple grew in different directions. He looked like after the divorce.

Susie and I joined Johnny on the couch. He was watching a show on termites. The bite mark that he left on his slice of pizza was a strange half-moon shape because one of his front teeth was missing.

Dad continued to puff on his cigarette. A few times, I glanced at him, even cleared my throat so that he might look at me and see my new shirt, but he didn't. He just kept working his rag over the brass.

A strong wind took the drapes: Mom's long dress. School's starting soon, and we're running late. Mom has me help her make eggs with turkey bacon while she talks on the phone with another professor. After she hangs up, she asks Johnny and me what we're going to do in school. "Nothing, Mom," I say. Johnny laughs.

Dad finished cleaning his saxophone and went to take a shower. Susie headed back into my room; her phone had beeped a few times. I thought about asking Johnny about Mom but decided not to. He seemed to be getting along better than I was. Why drag him into the cold? Instead, I put my arm around him. "We're okay, right?" I asked him. "Yeah, we're okay," I answered. He rubbed my hand.

* * *

Dylan's house was tucked away in an expensive neighborhood. All the homes had four-car garages and lawns big enough to play baseball. As Susie and I neared his house, a deep bass pummeled our bodies and rippled the side mirrors on Susie's Pontiac.

"This is the biggest one yet," Susie said.

"Don't the neighbors go crazy?" I asked.

"I heard Dylan buys them off."

We parked and headed inside. Furniture from each room had been moved to the side and covered with blankets. The living room was now a dance floor. I saw Bridgette dancing with a football player, her body swaying like tall grass. Her shirt was hiked up, showcasing her toned abs and pierced belly button. The kitchen had been turned into a bar. Stacks of red cups lined the counter, some so tall they drooped. There were silver cans of beer and bottles of rum, whiskey, vodka and other alcohols I hadn't seen before.

The backyard wasn't as crazy. It was cold out. Kids stared past the coastline, talking too soft to hear.

When I asked Susie what people were doing upstairs, she said, "All sorts of stuff," and giggled. "Let's get a drink," she said, her voice struggling to battle a rap song. Susie poured herself a vodka and cranberry. I did the same. The vodka totally wrecked the juice.

Some time later, Brandon Sweets and his friend arrived. Brandon said something, but it was too hard to hear and I didn't feel like saying "what." He grabbed a can of beer and headed upstairs with Susie.

I pulled out my cell phone and pretended to text.

"Hi," Brandon's friend said. "I'm Sebo."

"Hi," I said, closing my phone. "Is that short for Sebastian?"

"Yeah."

"Cool."

Sebo wasn't any taller than I was, but he was buff—his arms and chest looked filled with air, and every few seconds, he'd jerk his head to get the hair out of his eyes without touching it.

"Where are you from?" I asked, not knowing why I'd asked that.

"Around here." He grabbed a beer and played with the fuzz on his chin.

"Cool."

"I guess," he said. "Wanna go outside? I can barely hear what you're saying."

Some girls in my biology class stared at us. I could tell by their faces that they were shocked to see me talking to a guy they'd never seen before. I walked out behind Sebo into the cold night. There were a couple of chairs near the pool. We sat down. I didn't know if Sebo would like me outside—there weren't any distractions; it'd be all about me.

"Not a big fan of these parties," Sebo said as I dropped my hand into the pool. "Is it warm?"

"Very," I said. "I never like these parties either."

"I don't dance or anything, and I don't know anyone here, well, except for Brandon and Susie… and you."

We sat in the quiet for a long while, watching steam from the pool float into the air and block our view of each other.

"So how long have you known Susie?" Sebo said.

"A long time."

"Yeah, same here, with me and Brandon; he's like a brother."

"Yeah," I said, adjusting the latch of my necklace.

"Do you want another drink?" Sebo asked.

"Sure… a vodka and cranberry."

While Sebo was away, I pretended to text. I opened a blank message and began writing that I'd just met a cute guy. I even threw in some exclamation points and a couple smiley faces the way Mom did: Johnny, getting out of the car, pulling his wheelie backpack behind him like a miniature flight attendant. "Remember to drop the *e* in *love* before adding *i-n-g*," Mom says. "It's really the only tricky one on the test." Ten minutes later, Mom drops me off. Oldies play on the radio. I get out and look back and wave, but the sun is bright, so I can't see if she waves back.

Sebo returned with more beer and a large, red cup full of vodka.

"Not much cranberry left, so it's mostly vodka," he said.

Not wanting to look pathetic, I took a sip and did my best to hold it down.

"How is it?" Sebo asked.

"Strong." I coughed.

Sebo talked about soccer and how he was in the middle of varsity tryouts. He told me that he'd worked on his game by setting up cones at a nearby park and running with a weighted vest. I stared at Sebo's beat-up shell-top Adidas sneakers; he'd changed the laces from white to red and had them tied so that he could slip the shoes on and off.

"It's nice to talk to you," I said.

The silence felt heavy after those words. We just sat there.

"You smoke pot?" Sebo asked.

I never had, but I didn't want him to leave me. "A little."

"Cool. I have some in my truck. Come on."

He grabbed my hand and we sped through the house—too fast for me to see if the other girls noticed us. We squeezed into his truck. The leather was cold and the windows were tinted. I was hot and drunk.

Sebo clicked on the inside light and pulled out a book. Under the front cover were thin sheets of paper that looked like the kind Susie used to blot her oily skin. He placed two of the papers on his hairy knee and sprinkled in some pot.

When the lighter jumped out, Sebo smashed it to the tip and turned off the inside light. The only thing that was visible now was the red tip of the joint.

Sebo passed it to me. I pulled in the bitter smoke and coughed a few times.

He scooted over and I felt his right side press against my left side. The joint moved between us every two to three puffs. Between the alcohol and the weed, my body felt like melting wax. I even began to laugh at the scented pine tree that hung from his rearview mirror. He did too.

The joint finished, we sat, our breath heavy, the cabin cloudy. I closed my eyes. My head was quiet: Mr. Swink, the principal, coming into the classroom. I'm sitting at my desk with *The Stranger* flipped open, when he tells me to come with him. He looks sad, and when he sees I'm chewing gum, he doesn't tell me to spit it out like he normally does.

Sebo ran his fingers through my hair, down my neck and over my collar bone. I opened my eyes. I couldn't see his face, but could feel his humid breath. I'd been kissed once before—at a dance last year, but not like this, not in a truck at Dylan's party. This was something that Perfect Bridgette would do. The taste of his mouth was hot and smoky, and it made me sick. My head spun and my breath sped up.

I thought drinking and smoking would make me feel like Perfect Bridgette—and life always seemed easy for her. But it didn't. And I didn't feel good being with Sebo.

"I feel sick," I said.

"That's normal," Sebo said.

His hands rubbed my breasts. I tensed up. He headed south and began to unbutton my jeans. "No," I said, but he kept at it, trying his best to grab my zipper in the dark. "No," I said louder.

Since Mom had passed I'd heard my share of she's-up-there stuff, and I'd never really believed it, but what if she could see me or feel me the way I still could smell her and love her. She wouldn't want me to do this. She would want me to be home, be safe, be smart, and I wanted that too.

My stomach flipped. Vomit burned in the back of my throat. I kept it down. I coughed. Sebo told me to calm down. I felt the burn again; this time I couldn't hold it.

"Shit!" Sebo said, wiping vomit from his face.

I pulled the passenger door open and began to run away. My shoes banged the asphalt. The beep from Sebo's open truck door grew softer and softer. I tucked between two cars on a distant neighbor's driveway. I waited awhile, then walked down the road, letting the cold air whisper over my body.

The palm trees rustled and my heart began to steady. I opened my phone and called Susie. At the beep, I hesitated; the message recorded a few of my breaths before I hung up. *Where are you?* I texted her. She didn't text back. She was probably drunk and doing stuff with Brandon. My phone was probably beeping in her tight jeans that lay on the floor.

Sebo had seemed different—he had kind eyes. I thought he liked me.

Remembering Mrs. Z's big fingers tapping in her number, I found her name and pressed dial. It was 1:17 a.m., but she'd said to call anytime. She was going to ask me questions, questions that would make me look dumb. "Why were you in a car with a guy you didn't know?" she'd say. "Why aren't you being more careful?" she'd say. "Don't you know life is dangerous?" she'd say, mirroring one of the posters in her office—a picture of a gigantic wave about to swallow a ship. As if I didn't. As if I didn't know. The phone rang and rang. Her message clicked on—"Hi, you've reached Mrs. Zohorian. I'm not available right now. If you are experiencing a real emergency and have reached this voicemail..." I called again. Back to her fancy message.

The stars twinkled in the night sky: Mr. Swink hands me the phone in his office. Dad tells me about the accident. I picture glass glittering around Mom's totaled white Saab. Caution tape blocking off the street. Policemen taking pictures. Stoplights flashing red. I think about if we'd left later—thirty seconds, ten seconds, five seconds. I think about Mom sleeping in or Johnny spilling his juice like usual. I think about any accident that would've prevented hers.

I was far enough from Dylan's to no longer hear the music, just the sounds of leaves skipping over the pavement and the rush of traffic from the main road. I sat down on the curb and shivered. I called Dad. He never answered his cell, but it was worth a shot.

After the fifth ring, he picked up. He coughed a few times and knocked over a glass on his bedside table. "Shit," he said, then, "hello."

"Dad, it's me."

"Ella, what are you doing? It's late. You okay?"

"Could you pick me up?"

He coughed again and cleared his throat. "What? Sure. Where are you?"

"Seal Beach." I looked up at the street signs. "At the corner of PCH and Marina."

"Give me twenty minutes."

I thought I heard his belt buckle make noise as he slid on his pants.

"Okay," I said.

"Ella, let's stay on the phone, all right? I'm gonna put you right here—right in my shirt pocket."

I heard him go get Johnny out of bed, grab his keys, lock the front door, and start the car. Every couple minutes, he let me know where he was and how far he had to go. I listened to him hum; it was sweet and melodic. I couldn't remember the last time I'd heard him hum this tune—maybe all our eyes needed time to get used to the dark.

"You see me?" he said a little while later. Dad flashed his headlights and pulled alongside the curb. I opened the car door and got in. Johnny was in the back, with his red blanket, asleep. "You look cold," Dad said, taking off his coat and handing it over. "What the hell happened?"

"Sorry," I said, putting on Dad's already-warm coat.

"Tomorrow we'll talk," Dad said, putting the car in gear. "Right now I'm tired and Johnny's sleeping. But you need to be safer, okay? My girl's sure as hell not gonna be wandering the streets at one in the morning."

I nodded and closed my eyes. In a strange way, it felt good to hear him angry. I liked that he wanted me to be safe.

"But I'm happy you called, Ella. I am. You know who this is?" Dad said, pointing to the radio.

"No," I said.

"You're named after her."

"Ella Fitzgerald," I said.

He smiled.

That was a new question, one besides "How was school?"

We began to climb the hill that led to the Vincent Thomas Bridge, a suspension bridge that connected Long Beach and San Pedro. At night it wore little blue sparkling lights.

Rain started falling. I listened to drops tap the roof of the car. "Remember when you were real little and whenever it would rain, you, me and Mom would jump in the car and go for a ride?"

"Yeah," I said, shoving my right hand into the pocket of Dad's jacket where my fingers came into contact with a sharp piece of paper. As I started to pull it out, I saw *Dad* written on the front in large, loopy cursive. It was the envelope from Mrs. Z's office. I'd left it in my jeans and Dad must have done laundry. My face burned. I couldn't believe that I'd been so dumb, that I hadn't thrown it away. I shoved it deep down into the pocket, felt the paper squish and crinkle.

The lights that lit up the bridge sliced through the windows as we drove. The Vincent Thomas's frame was made up of hundreds of metal triangles, making me think of geometry and the "real world" problems from class. Mr. Nguyen had told us that the triangle was the strongest shape, which was why it was used in construction.

Out the windshield, raindrops fell into the shafts of our headlights, while inside a steady beat trickled from the car speakers: Mom, sitting in this cracked leather seat, purse on her lap, auburn hair resting on her shoulders, a small smile on her face. I wondered whether Dad could see mine, my own small smile, maybe out of the corner of his eye.

I clutched the necklace and rested my head against the cold window. We headed north, over puddles and under rain.

A DAY LIKE TODAY

* * *

Locklin pulled up alongside the curb, behind other cars, and finished his cigarette. His old oil-spattered spot on the driveway was now occupied by Roger's car—a shiny red Mercedes coupe, brand new, no plates, and no oil leak.

The sun was out, but it was cold, a typical winter day in Venice. Locklin drew a deep breath before heading to the trunk to fetch his son Will's birthday present. He'd done the best he could without wrapping paper, using just a few sheets of aluminum foil, shiny-side up.

As he walked to the front door, he remembered moving into this house, installing a new garage door, buying sod for the yard, and hanging Christmas lights along the roofline.

Locklin had always been so mild-mannered, a person always going out of his way to avoid trouble. He took the split, and resulting divorce with Melanie well, hoping all the while that holding his head up would make things better, but it hadn't.

He stood atop the welcome mat and rang the bell. Melanie pulled the door open so casually, like he was the mailman. "Hi," she said. Her lips were bright red and she looked well-rested. Her hair was shorter, the ends cut at a flattering angle. "Come in," she said. The floorboards creaked in familiar spots and books lived on the same shelves, but different keys sat in the blue bowl, and new shoes lay on the floor by the hallway closet. Locklin stared at a pair of big, coffee-colored loafers.

Melanie walked Locklin to the kitchen, where he set his gift down. They sat at the breakfast nook. Someone's plate was finished and the egg yolk had dried.

"How's work?" Melanie said.

"Yeah," Locklin said. "Doing some handyman stuff right now: painting, plumbing, a bit of electrical work. You look nice, Mel."

Melanie sipped her coffee and wadded up a napkin.

"Where's Roger?" Locklin asked. "Saw his new car out front."

"Took the van to pick up Will and his friends. There was a sleepover."

"At Lloyd's house?"

"Floyd. His friend's name is Floyd," Melanie said, pouring some more cream into her coffee.

"It's weird that a little kid's named Floyd… isn't it?"

"How's your new place?"

"Pretty nice. Quiet, you know."

Locklin thought about saying "I miss you" but decided against it. He'd done it before and the words usually sat in the air like an unpleasant odor. Not too long after, Roger pulled into the driveway, and Locklin took a few sips of watered-down coffee until the door swung open. With it came a flood of noise: Will, Will's friends, Roger, and Roger's collie, Figgy, whose nails made little tapping sounds on the hardwood.

"Happy birthday, sweetie," Melanie said as Will turned the corner. He smiled. "I can't believe you're already nine!"

Figgy barked a couple more times and his collar jingled. Will's friends laughed.

"Hi, buddy," Locklin said, lifting Will and squeezing him tightly. He always smelled so clean and young, and Locklin took a long draw before setting his boy back down.

"Dad," he said, "it's my golden birthday."

"A what?"

Roger approached and said, "It's when the date matches your age." He then patted Locklin on the shoulder.

"Yeah," Will said, "today I'm nine on the ninth." Some of his hair was stuck to his forehead and crumbs of sleep sat in the corners of his eyes.

Everyone took a seat in the living room. Locklin stared at the pile of ash that rested in the fireplace and at the dog hair that coated the couch. It would have been smart, Locklin thought, to strategize exactly how he was going to hurt Roger. He'd certainly had plenty of time to think of something, but that was the problem with nice guys—they spent so much of their lives avoiding trouble that when it came time to make some, they didn't know how. Locklin sometimes thought about the perfect world: the one with Roger driving too fast on a slick highway, the radio loud, his shiny coupe tucked in the blindspot of an eighteen-wheeler. It'd go fast—something sudden, on impact. Melanie would be saddened, and he'd be there for her. Will would be shocked, and he'd console. To Locklin, revenge always sounded good. Many times, he heard people argue against the death penalty, saying, "Sure, it kills the murderer, but it doesn't bring the victim back. Revenge doesn't pay off." But he didn't buy that—he bet that some people close to the victim felt relieved when the perpetrator was strapped to the table and pumped full of fluid.

"Good to see you," Roger said to Locklin. His blue eyes stood out against his tanned skin, and his curly hair was stiff with hairspray.

"Good to be seen," Locklin said.

"How's work going?"

"Incredible."

"Good, good. I just got a new car. Really great ride."

Melanie stood up. "So I thought we'd start off by having a little lunch. I made a few different things—some eggs and bacon for those who want a late breakfast, and then there are some sandwiches. I even grabbed a couple pepperoni pizzas."

Floyd said he was going to put eggs and bacon on a slice of pizza and a couple boys, including Will, said, "Eww." Figgy barked again and a little drool drizzled over his black lips.

Everyone headed to the kitchen and helped themselves. Locklin just wanted another cup of coffee. He opened the cabinets—cabinets he'd built—and tried to find the World's Best Dad mug that Will had bought him a couple of Christmases ago, but it was no longer around. He settled on a plain white one, sat at the table, and stared out the window onto his old street. It was a day like today, a cold day with sun high, when Melanie had come home from work and told him that she didn't love him anymore, that she'd been seeing someone, a guy named Roger. The strange thing was, Locklin wasn't angry with Melanie. He wanted so much to hate her, but he couldn't. Years of love couldn't be transformed into anything else. Instead, Roger became the target of all his quiet rage: jobs that hadn't worked out, people who were disrespectful, dishonest, racist, and ugly. To Locklin, all these things were connected to Roger. In so many ways, though, Roger was the man he wanted to be—handsome, richer, better educated. He just never thought that Melanie wanted him to be these things, too, and moreover, he knew he couldn't be. Each time the two men saw each other—in the early going, anyhow—Roger always extended his hairy hand for a shake, and Locklin couldn't help but think that *this* was the hand that now got to hang ornaments, flip the pages of Will's bedtime stories, and pull Melanie's soft panties down, over her thighs and knees, calves and subtly-rounded ankles.

After a while, everyone joined Locklin at the table. Roger ate his bacon with a fork and knife; Melanie blotted her pizza with a napkin, and Will picked off shiny pepperonis and popped them into his mouth. Melanie touched Roger's hand after she finished her slice, and Locklin found himself staring at Roger's sun-spotted face.

The worst part about divorce was when one of the parties remarried, the other had to witness all the stages of love unfold. Melanie and Roger had been together for a year now—meeting at church of all places—and Locklin knew that the proposal was coming. He could sense it. If Roger were a friend of his, he'd say to go for it. What'd it matter, though?—the two of them were already living together, sharing a bed, a house, a life.

The kids laughed as Floyd finished telling a story about how he got sent home for having lice, and Roger got up and made a fire. When Roger returned to the table, he whispered something into Will's ear, and Will rushed down the hall and came back with a box the size of Figgy. "Told him he could open one now," Roger said to Melanie.

"Okay," she said, "just one."

The fire began to catch and pop.

Will tore through the wrapping paper and Locklin watched scraps flutter to the floor. "No way!" Will said. "It's the remote-control plane I wanted!"

"A P-51 Mustang!" Floyd said.

"So cool!" said another one of Will's friends, a short one with Velcro shoes.

Melanie stared at Will and narrowed her eyes. Will then

headed over to Roger, laying his head flat against his cashmere sweater. "Thanks, Roger," he said.

"Glad you like it," Roger said. "It's the best one on the market, so be careful. And good news... I charged it up this morning so all you have to do is slide it out. It's ready."

"Surprised he didn't have a Marine come over to show Will how to fly it," Locklin said to Floyd, who just shrugged his shoulders.

Will and his friends got up and darted to the street. Figgy followed.

Roger and Melanie walked across the room and gazed out the large bay window. The fire was going strong now, consuming the wood and leaving parts of it incandescent. They then plopped on the couch. "Will never saw it coming," Melanie said, propping her feet on Roger's lap.

"Well, I saw him looking at it at the store, and later I saw him looking at it on the computer," he said, rubbing her smooth heels.

Locklin didn't understand why they had to be so affectionate.

He lifted the box that lay next to the table. "Made in China," he said. "Crazy to think that an all-American plane like the P-51 would someday be made by the Chinese."

Roger laughed a little, working his hands around Melanie's ankles that bore cuts from a recent shave. The fire hissed as flames encountered some moisture in the wood.

There was a loud whirling sound. "Look at it," Melanie said. She and Roger stood and moved towards the window and watched the plane fly. Locklin didn't budge. He stared at the fire. So much of his life had been pretending he was happy when he wasn't, and he wondered where he'd be today if he'd *always* told the truth—if he'd had the courage to tell his father to pull himself together, or the boldness to tell his mom to stop popping pills, or if he could just tell Melanie how much he still loved her and how he'd ruin everything just for another night with her.

Roger brought his hand out from his pocket and wrapped his thumb through one of Melanie's belt loops. Locklin remembered doing that while standing in the garden at Paul Connick's home when Melanie told him that she'd gotten pregnant. And he remembered telling her he'd find a way to make it work.

Later, the kids and Figgy came inside. Will held the plane under his arm and Roger told him to be more careful. Floyd carried the joystick and others talked about how great it was when the wind came along and pushed the P-51 into "warp speed."

"So, how was it?" Melanie asked.

Will smiled. Many of his grown-up teeth had come in and were too big for his mouth. "Gonna go recharge it," he said, heading down the hall with his friends.

"Nine years old," Locklin said. "I remember being in the delivery room. He had this huge glob of black hair. The nurse even made a joke about Elvis."

"While they're in there," Melanie said, "let's get the cake ready." She opened the fridge and pulled out a slab of cake—chocolate with blue icing piped along the borders. Roger plucked nine candles from the junk drawer and placed them in a circle around the words HAPPY BIRTHDAY WILL. Locklin pulled out his lighter, spun the flint wheel, and dragged the fire over the wicks.

When the boys came out from Will's bedroom, Roger, Melanie, and Locklin started singing. Will smiled and came to the table, his face only inches from the icing. His eyes were open wide, enough for Locklin to see flames reflected in his boy's pupils. With a big breath, Will extinguished all the candles and rings of smoke curled to the popcorn ceiling.

As Locklin divvied up the cake, he thought about cutting another cake a long time ago, in that Marriot ballroom packed with friends and family from high school. Melanie's hair was blondish then, and she wore a loose dress to hide the bump.

Locklin sat next to Will in front of the fireplace. The brick was warm and Locklin put his arm around his boy. He was proud of the way Will had handled it all—he seemed okay, not blaming himself or anything. Will was a lot like he was, though, and that worried him. Once, Locklin had talked to him about how there were two types of people in this world: volcanoes and geysers. "Volcanoes, like you and me," he'd said, "sit and brew and stuff all their problems. The thing is, one day, they erupt. You don't know how or when, but when it happens, it's ugly. It's best to be like your mother, a geyser—let it out often and easily. Don't hold back." Will had seemingly understood.

The fire was hot on his back, so Locklin got up and walked the hall to the bathroom. A new bed sat in his old room, a four-poster thing, unmade, the sheets messy and showcasing the bodily imprints from the night before. Once inside the bathroom, he pulled the door shut and opened the medicine cabinet, timing a cough with the squeak of a hinge. The spot where Locklin's shaving brush used to sit had been taken over by a curvy black bottle of aftershave. BOSS, the label read. Locklin held the bottle over the toilet and added some piss to it, then returned the BOSS to its proper spot.

Before reaching the living room, Locklin peeked into Will's room. The Dodgers banner that Locklin had bought him a few months ago hung above his bed, and a team photo of the Raiders was still tacked to the closet door. On the bookshelf was a photo of Locklin and Will setting up a tent. The sun hit the picture in the afternoon and it was beginning to yellow. The P-51 Mustang charged on the bed. Next to it was a card from Roger: *Dear Billy,* it read, *May you have a beautiful birthday. I love spending time with you. –Dad*

Locklin read the card again. He imagined Will calling Roger "Dad." His neck stiffened and his limbs burned.

With everyone in the living room talking, occupied, still shoving cake into their mouths, Locklin picked up the P-51, inspected the wings and tail, popped off the engine cover and looked inside at all the wires and gears. He brought out his screwdriver keychain and with a couple quick turns, loosened the propeller, then headed back to the living room.

"Hun," Roger said, "you want me to put some more logs on the fire?"

"Please," Melanie said.

Locklin grabbed a beer and sat on the couch. The kids were laughing. The dog barked at something on the back porch. He pictured quiet Meadow Road, saw the P-51 tracing through the winter air, then losing control, veering, dropping, exploding against the asphalt, leaving behind shiny shards to sparkle in the afternoon sun.

Melanie straightened up the kitchen and Roger dropped another log onto the fire. Will and his pals were on the floor, listening to Floyd talk about one of his teachers at school: "I swear," he said, "she has this thing on her cheek, a mole or something, and there's this huge hair that grows from it. And whenever she uses the projector, it blows around because of the fan!" The kids laughed hard.

"You think it's charged up?" Will asked.

"Probably," Floyd said.

The kids rushed to the bedroom.

"The light's blinking!"

They took the plane outside. Melanie, Roger, Figgy, and Locklin followed. Will set the plane down at the south end of Meadow Road. The kids were excited, talking over one another and telling Will what he should do. Locklin stood still, hands deep in his pockets, a light smile on his face.

"Watch this," Will said. "I was reading the manual. Gonna make it do a barrel roll."

"Be careful," Roger said.

"Yes," Melanie said. "Be careful, sweetie."

"Let it rip," said Floyd.

"Go for it," said Locklin, running his tongue over his beer-soaked lips.

Will slammed the joystick up and the tires hummed as they spun along the pavement. When the plane moved fast enough, a little light blinked on the joystick, telling the "pilot" that it was ready for take-off. Will pressed the button and the plane lifted, flying over a car, a stop sign, a two-story house, and then an old maple. It flew northward until Will brought it back around towards the house. He was calling out his movements, and Floyd was repeating them in a garbled voice that was supposed to sound like a walkie-talkie. "All right," Will said, "gonna attempt a roll." Then Floyd said it: "Attempting barrel roll. All clear."

Melanie held Roger's hand, her thin fingers intertwined with his thick ones. Early after Locklin and Melanie separated, her ring finger had a tan line from where her wedding band used to sit, and that always made Locklin happy—made him feel that even nature was on his side. But now, that sliver of skin had found the sun.

Will twisted a few knobs on the joystick and, just then, the propeller flew off and skipped across the pavement. The ping grew softer and softer as it made its way down the road.

"Oh, no," Floyd said.

The P-51 began to wobble like a fat duck and nosedived straight down at a home, shattering as it crashed into a neighbor's chimney.

"Jesus!" Roger said. "What the hell? What did you do?"

"Nothing," Will said. "I was just doing it like normal and the propeller flew off."

"Flew off," Roger said. His neck turned red. "It's brand new!"

"I swear," Will said, his lips quivering.

Locklin couldn't believe what he'd done. When he'd looked at the plane, he'd seen Roger, never Will.

"Unbelievable!" Roger said.

Will's friends backed away, as did Figgy, but Locklin approached and put his hand on Roger's shoulder. "That's enough. It's just a toy."

"A *toy*! It's just a *toy* because *I* bought it."

Will stared at the street and a gust blew strongly, causing him to shut his eyes. He kept them closed long after the wind passed, doing all he could to keep from crying in front of his friends.

Melanie came to Roger's side and used a softer voice. "It's okay," she said. "We can just buy him a new one. It's no big deal."

"A new one!" Roger said. "That's it—let Roger buy him a new one."

When Melanie touched Roger, he shooed her off.

Will looked up for the first time in a while and Roger stared directly at him. "I knew I shouldn't have bought this for you," he said. "I knew you'd screw up. You always screw up."

"Watch your mouth," Locklin said. "Don't talk to Will like that."

Melanie froze.

Will stood straighter and looked at his father with big eyes. Locklin's fingers twitched and his muscles tightened. He didn't know what his next move was, but he could feel his son's gaze, and it was the only bit of warmth that had been flung his way in quite some time. He listened to bursts of breath hiss through his nostrils and took another step towards Roger.

Roger didn't move.

Locklin stared into his eyes.

Every other feature on Roger's face seemed to blur and, for the first time, Locklin thought Roger looked scared. When you reduced a person to just his eyes, just those little circles of color, everyone looked young and frightened.

Locklin bent his fingers and felt his dirty nails dig into his palm. In a soft voice, he said, "Haven't you hurt me enough? You take my wife, my house, my bedroom, and you insult my son." He could feel his heartbeat in his neck and beads of sweat sprout on his brow.

Roger closed his eyes and clenched his teeth, as if expecting to be hit at any moment.

"Dad," Will said, coming to his father's side. "Don't! Please. It's okay, really."

Roger opened his eyes and both men turned towards Will. The boy's skin was flushed and he held his hands together, begging.

No one wanted to move, but when Melanie started back towards the house, Roger and Figgy followed, and eventually, all the children surrounded Will and their voices reached their normal volumes.

Locklin stood there, watching his breath fog up the cold air. He pulled out a cigarette and lit up. In his old home's front window, he saw Melanie and Roger fighting. She was waving her arms and pointing outside, and Roger was standing still, shaking his head.

"Hey, guys," Locklin said to Will's friends. "Do me a favor. Go grab my present for Will. It's in the kitchen, I think. The one wrapped in aluminum foil."

The kids took off.

With everyone gone, Locklin sat next to his son on the curb. Goosebumps dotted Will's arms, and Locklin ran his hand over them. "You okay, buddy?" he asked.

"Yeah," Will said, placing his head on his father's chest.

Locklin listened to the sigh of nearby traffic, studied the long shadows of oaks on the pavement, and continued to rub his boy's smooth forearms. "Can't believe how big you're getting," he said.

"I'll be as big as you soon," Will said.

"Bigger," Locklin said. "Much bigger." He drew a deep breath and looked up at the cloudless sky. With his cigarette finished, he flicked the butt onto the road and watched it smolder for a few seconds. Again, the wind picked up, and Locklin did his best to shield his boy. They sat there, faces tight, eyes narrowed, huddled, waiting for the gust to pass through.

DISSONANCE

* * *

Mick hadn't been this close since he was six years old.

He sat in his car, inspecting her house, studying the white paint job, large windows, and untamed bougainvillea that crept across the top of her garage door. An olive tree drooped in her front yard and the wind tickled each branch, causing the shadows that it cast on her driveway to dance.

A classical music station played inside his car. Mick took a sip of his coffee, which had now gone cold. He listened to Schubert's "Sonata in A Minor," a somber piece that he'd put on the auditory part of the final exam he'd given to his students last week, just before school had gotten out for summer vacation.

Mick wanted to see her, talk to her, feel the scar on her right knee, remind her he was alive, that he'd survived after what she'd put him through, and let her know that she'd made him live a pianissimo life instead of the forte one he desired.

It'd be twenty-nine years tomorrow since she'd left Mick and his father. He'd done his best to squelch the memory, sought treatment with MDs and taken yellow pills that seemed big as marbles, but it was tattooed in his mind—her big blue eyes, her gray skirt that was pleated like a Japanese fan, her light soapy smell, and her rust-colored hair that sat in a pile atop her head. He could see her skinny fingers remove her keys from the hook in the foyer. "Can I come?" Mick remembered saying.

"You should stay here," she said, looking at him with her shiny eyes.

"Where are you going, Mom?"

"To the store."

"Can you get me some lemonade?"

"Sure, Mickey," she said, adjusting the ladybug brooch on her chunky cardigan.

She never came back. That was it, the last time Mick saw her, saw her back as she flung her purse over her shoulder and navigated the walkway with her black shoes.

Mick's dad called the police. He filed a report. He sat on the couch. "She'll be home soon," he said. "Everything will be okay." But Mick remembered thinking it wouldn't be.

When Mick got older and asked about her, his father said, "She couldn't handle this life. She wasn't ready for this, for us," then he changed the subject and walked in the other direction. Mick's dad never dated again, and did his best to wear a smile and act as if nothing had happened.

The young Mick hated that his father faked happiness in the hopes that it would stick, but as an adult, Mick admired him for living a minor life in the hopes of making his major.

Last month, Mick had worn a black suit, buried his father, and tossed a handful of dirt onto a varnished casket. He walked away from the service an orphan with a significant bequest which he'd used to hire a private detective. The detective had found her address: She was only forty-eight miles away, their two homes only a pinky nail apart on the map.

Wind powered through her suburban street and leaves scurried along the pavement in a staccato-like manner. Her home's features fed his imagination, and he pictured her walking the brick path, saw her hand lifting the mailbox flag, and envisioned her fingers twisting the door knob.

Chopin's "Ballade Numero Un" trickled from the car speakers, each black and white key stroke delivering a punch. Mick closed his eyes and placed his head against the headrest; she used to play this song in the living room. "Feel the emotion, Mickey. Feel the sadness," she used to say. He would sit next to her on the piano bench and watch her hands brush the keys and her feet pump the golden pedals. He remembered her teaching him the first few notes on her baby grand Steinway that could also be used as a player-piano, the one that Mick now had in his home. "Remember this, Mickey... this trick will help you with line notes—E, G, B, D, F—'Every good boy does fine.'"

Having had enough for one day, Mick put his car in gear and

sped off, but not more than a few houses away from hers, he noticed a "For Lease" sign planted in a neighbor's lawn. He parked the car and got out, grabbed a flyer and toured the home from the outside—two stories, a large garage, and a few orange trees in the front yard. Each of the windows wore navy shutters and some of the paint was flaking. The flyer called it *charming* and *rustic* and *a handyman's dream,* all real-estate synonyms for *breaking down.*

Mick returned to his car and took off. With the gas tank nearing empty, he pulled into a station and filled up. While he pumped, he combed the flyer; he could afford the place, especially with the recent bequest. He pulled out his cell phone and dialed.

"L.A. Rentals and Services," the voice on the other side said. Mick could practically smell the perfume through the receiver. He talked to the lady about the house. "It's a great home," she said. "A beautiful place with great neighbors."

Mick took it.

* * *

The next morning, the movers arrived and Mick let them pack, only giving them one instruction: "Be careful with the Steinway. It's very old."

He drove to his new house to meet the real-estate agent. She was already in the driveway on his arrival, wearing a yellow business suit with a white blouse. She dangled the keys to his new home like a dog's treat. As they shook hands, her bracelets clashed. Everything she said seemed to be followed by an exclamation point, even routine stuff like *sign here* and *initial there.* "Do you want a tour?" she said.

"It's all right," Mick said. "I'll figure it out."

"Easiest client ever," she said.

They completed the paperwork, and she hopped back into her little red convertible and sped off, tapping the horn twice.

Mick opened the front door easily, too easily, as the locking mechanism didn't work.

Inside the house, a heavy scent of mildew hung in the hallways. He explored the floor plan and lumbered up to the second story, where he honed in on her home from a bedroom. Mick was so close to the window that his breath fogged up the glass.

A car pulled into her driveway. A tall, bearded man and a teenager got out. The teenager was wearing a baseball uniform that was streaked with mud and grass stains, while the bearded man wore a newsboy cap and a blue flannel shirt. The man opened the gate and the two of them walked to the front door. Mick hoped to get a look at her and see if his imagination's depiction matched reality's, but he didn't get the chance as the teenager and the man let themselves in and closed the door behind them.

Mick pulled up a chair that had been left behind and continued to stare through the large bedroom window that was sliced up by panes. Not only have I been left… I've been replaced, he thought.

He went to his car and removed a few boxes, brought them into the house, and placed them on the floor. One thing about moving, he realized, was that he kept everything, finding an old student's end-of-semester review that for some reason he'd saved: *Music doesn't just seem to be Dr. Raskowski's job. It seems to be his life. You can tell that he lives in music. When speaking of certain pieces, he seems to ache with emotion.* He also found an étude he'd begun to write a few years ago, though he'd given up on it when he couldn't compose the proper ending. He inspected his piece, hummed it, and added a few notes. As he transferred a biography of Chopin from box to shelf, he opened the book to the flyleaf: *I think you love Chopin as much as I love you. Yours forever, -Lisa.* He thought about his ex-fiancée, and the way she'd called off the wedding last year, telling him he was distrusting and paranoid, and that she'd never done anything to deserve his suspicion. He dusted off a few more books and mapped out where he'd put his furniture.

The movers arrived a couple hours later. Mick watched them place the Steinway on a dolly and wheel it to the front door. "Right here," Mick said, as they came in. "Right here in the living room." He picked a spot near the back of the home where two large windows came together and looked out onto the backyard. Wanting to test out the new notes he'd written, he placed his sheet music on the stand and hunched over the piano. Not crazy about it, he played something else, an oeuvre by Handel.

Some time later, the movers finished up and drove off. Mick walked back up the stairs and let his eyes burn into her home, noticing that the car the man and the teenager had arrived in was gone.

Near his bed, the movers had placed a box marked *fragile*. In it were some records and his father's gold wrist watch that he'd sometimes tried on as a child. Back then, it was so large that it wrapped his wrist like a hula-hoop, but now it fit. The metal was cold and the face was scratched, and he couldn't help but wonder how many times his father had looked at the watch, the numbers, the big and little hands, and thought, How long has it been? When is she coming back?

Mick slid off the watch and placed it next to his bed. He decided to take a walk. Outside, the air was warm, a typical Los Angeles summer night. Heat from the black asphalt rose into Mick's shoes, and a light breeze washed over him and he savored it. Her outdoor lights were on, but inside the home was black. What if I knocked right now? Mick thought... just pulled the gate open and knocked a couple times. Would she recognize me?

The sky was clear. A plane's lights blinked as it flew across the darkness. At first glance, Mick believed it to be a shooting star, and even when he realized it wasn't, he still made a wish.

At the end of the street, a home was illuminated. Inside, a family played a board game, laughed, rolled dice, and moved tokens.

He headed back home and brushed his teeth. He wondered if she ever thought about that "going to the store" day, if they ever thought of one another at the same time, if their thoughts crossed where their paths hadn't.

He lolled on his bed and stared at the popcorn ceiling. He thought of his father and the way he'd died in the hospital a few months ago. He was strong up until the end. "We had a good run, didn't we?" he asked Mick one day.

"We did."

"We defied the odds. Just remember that. We made it." He tried his best to laugh a little laugh, but it just came out as a cough. "You remember those nights of omelets for dinner? You remember the Mustang I bought you?"

"Yes."

"We had a good time. We had a good time. We had a good time," Mick's dad said, each sentence softer than the one before it.

* * *

The next morning, Mick drove to different stores around town, picked up tools that were needed to fix the front door, banister and leaky faucets, and bought groceries to fill the refrigerator.

When he returned home and removed the bags from his trunk, a neighbor, with a skinny frame and pale face, was watering his flowers along the property line. "Howdy, I'm Ray," he said.

Mick set his bags down and walked over. "Mick."

The two men shook hands.

"Welcome to the neighborhood," Ray said, moving his thumb over the opening of the hose to soften the stream. "This is a great place to live. Really nice. How do you like your home?"

"Well, there's a lot of work to be done."

"Yeah, it's got a nice view though, right?"

"I guess."

"So what brings you to this little town?" Ray said, picking at a scab on his elbow. "I feel like everyone around here is either starting up or starting over. Which one are you?"

"Not sure yet."

"Well, happy to know you," Ray said. He started telling Mick about the neighbors. When he got to her house, he said: "Juliette lives there. She's an older lady who's been here by herself for a long time. A real sweet woman. You'll like her."

Mick nodded.

Seconds passed. The two men listened to the water saturate the ground.

"Well, I better get going, don't want to overwater this area," said Ray. "Take care, Mick. It was great to meet you."

"Likewise," Mick said, heading back to his car, playing the sound bites: by herself… long time… sweet woman. He put the food away and began to work on the front door. Before long, dusk arrived and slowly stole light from the sky.

While he worked, he listened to the player-piano perform a Chopin piece. He relished the dark bass chords and the sweeter notes from the treble clef.

Mick continued to tweak the door, unfasten screws and change parts, and then he tested his work, pulling the door closed, hoping it would stay shut. The latch clicked. The door held.

He took a break, went to the piano, ran his hands over the ivory keys that had yellowed, and played Chopin's "Prelude in E Minor." Mick liked the syrupy darkness that it conveyed. He played it again and again, analyzed the soft beginning, the haunting middle, and the abrupt and disconcerting finale.

The doorbell sounded. Mick got up, walked to the foyer, and pulled the door open.

"Yes," he said.

It was she.

Certainly time had altered her features and loosened her skin, and made her look harder than the character he'd created in his mind, but even in the final obscuring minutes of dusk, he knew. She stood on the welcome mat that had been left by the previous owner; the word *welcome,* beaten and eroded by the sun.

His fingers began to twitch as they did when he first started performing at piano competitions in grade school, and his heartbeat's tempo accelerated from moderato to presto.

"Hi," she said, a word so routine yet unfamiliar. "My name is Juliette. I live across the street." She turned and pointed to her house. "The one over there with the picket fence and olive tree."

"Mom," he thought about saying. "Mom, it's me—Mickey," but the words were so foreign, that his mouth couldn't grip them. He inspected her knee-length pleated skirt that showcased the scar she'd suffered, the one Mick used to run his hand over while watching TV. Her hair was no longer the color of rust, but now of steel wool, and her feet, those veiny feet that had walked out, were strapped into leather sandals.

"Anyway," she said. "I made you a pie."

She wouldn't even let him have his day. He'd moved in across the street. He was biding his time, waiting for a moment when a rush of confidence would blow into his chest, but she had to surprise him on his stoop.

Mick had wanted this moment since that sunny lemonade afternoon. So many times he'd imagined the scenario: her face, the place, his words, which changed depending on his mood. Sometimes he screamed, told her how he pedaled his bike to every grocery store and asked about her; other times they hugged, kissed, and cried. But not once in all his scenarios had she not recognized him. Not once had he not a thing to say. As Mick held the door open and gazed into her shiny eyes, he froze—worried he'd be rejected again. If he couldn't keep her in his youth, why would she want him now? He had lived with one rejection, but another would make him believe there wasn't a note of remorse.

"Did I hear you playing piano?" she asked.

Mick drew a deep breath. "Yes."

"Was that Chopin?"

"Yes."

She tucked a piece of grayish hair behind her ear. "You can taste the despair in it, can't you? I used to play piano, a very long time ago."

The two of them stood close enough to touch but with little reason to do so.

"Well," she said, "it was nice chatting with you. Welcome to the neighborhood. I hope you enjoy the pie."

She turned around and left.

He stood in his doorway, the golden-brown pie in his hands, the rich blueberries oozing from crannies. The dish was still warm, and Mick let some of the heat transfer to his hands. A better neighbor than she was a mother, he thought, listening to the decrescendo of her steps as she walked down his steep driveway and out of sight.

ONE-NIGHT STAND

* * *

I pulled out behind some numbnut whose blinker had been flashing since the Reagan administration. One day he'd turn left, just not today. I was on my way to perform at Koffee Korner's open mic in North Hollywood, not the best comedy venue, but one where I didn't have to kiss anyone's ass for stage time. The drive went fast, as I replayed my set in my head, working through jokes.

Earlier in the day, my girlfriend, Meredith, had said, "Just think about it… I love that you do comedy, but this job's only a few hours a day, mostly in the early afternoon, and you'll have health insurance. Just think about it." *Just think about it…* every man knew that was woman for *when's it gonna make sense to you?* Meredith's brother had just secured a job as the manager of a Costco in Culver City and he was in charge of hiring. I just couldn't picture myself wearing that little red vest, though, absorbing all that fluorescent light day after day, helping sell crates of mayo, or tons of tins of sardines, or bundles of bidets, or whatever the hell went down in those gigantic warehouses.

I arrived at Koffee Korner, got out, put six coins in the meter (one Canadian piece), made sure my fly was zipped up, and entered.

"What's up, Gray? You want something to drink?" said the barista. Her hair was short and she wore a gold ring in her left nostril.

"Nothing strong enough back there."

"You'll be fine," she said.

"That's probably what Siegfried told Roy before his last show."

"Sure you don't want something?"

"Do you have one of those Mexican cokes—the ones in the bottle? At least I can get ten cents outta this if all else fails."

"Think it's only five in California," she said, passing over the caffeinated sugar.

I plopped down on a couch that wasn't even good enough for Goodwill and watched two guys set up. They plugged extension cords into power strips and moved chairs and cleared tables. The "stage" was in the middle of the coffee shop, a round thing that made it possible to bomb from every angle. The two men lifted a small aquarium. I wondered how many shitty jokes and folk songs the fish had been subjected to—maybe the fake treasure and booty they swam above helped curb their anger. I also wondered how come the chubby orange one looked so much like my Uncle Dom.

Sweet nervousness coated my body. I could feel my heart beat strongly and the tips of my fingers twitch, but I was used to it by now; it was actually a good thing. I'd read about a comic—maybe Steve Martin, maybe Steven Wright—who vomited before every show, and if he didn't vomit he knew he was in for a bad night, so I savored my anxiety, found it refreshing, normal. That's what I loved so much about comedy—it was about being human, feeling insecure, examining life's hardship. It was the opposite of real life... where everyone lied about their happiness, their marriage, their job, where everyone tattooed smiles atop their frowns.

"Gray? That you, chief?" said Jim, the owner. He wore a beanie and chewed on a health bar.

"Hey, Jim. How are ya?"

"Glad you're performing tonight."

"Yeah," I said. I wondered when he'd start talking to me about his daughter.

"How's it been goin'?"

"Okay. Still trying to get a good five-minute set."

"Hey, have you called Natalie?"

Consistent as a morning piss, I thought. "No, I have a wonderful girlfriend. How many women would put up with someone who does this all the time? She even helps me with jokes—jokes about *her*."

"I don't mean it like that. You two could be friends. You know, go to dinner, see movies..."

"I don't even do that with *my* lady."

"Just call her, Gray. Come on. She likes you." He ripped a fluorescent yellow flyer down from the corkboard. Staples discharged. He penned her number on the back. "Take it," he said, sitting down next to me. Peanuts from the bar flew out of his mouth as he chewed. Some of them landed on my pants. We both stared at the crumbs for a few seconds before he brushed them off my leg with the flyer. "Seriously, Gray. Take it." He folded the paper and slid it in my jacket pocket. His cell sounded. The ring was a Zeppelin tune. "Be right back," he said.

I pulled the flyer out from my jacket. Most times, I felt a sense of accomplishment when capturing a lady's phone number, but when it was pushed onto you by her spitting father, well, it felt like an arranged marriage. I needed to get rid of this number. I could hear Meredith: "Wait, her *dad* gave you her number? What? Dads don't give away numbers. My dad still wouldn't give you *my* number and we've been together for a year."

I put the phone number in my empty Coke bottle and threw it away. Thinking of Meredith made me think of her brother, which made me think of Costco, which made me think of long lines and oily pizza and someone shouting, "Gray, price check on the 600-pound box of tampons!" I pulled out my wallet, opened the billfold, and plucked out Meredith's brother's business card. The paper was thick and his name, Carl Martin, was slanted slightly to the right as if a strong wind was pushing it eastward. The corners had been bent and each letter in STORE MANAGER was slightly raised. I ran my thumb across the words; in Braille, they spelled failure.

Jim was still on the phone. "Perfect, perfect," he said, then hung up. "Oh, man," he said, coming over to me. "Got some good news for you, Gray. Guess what just happened?"

"You sold off your daughter?"

"No. Guess again."

"You're getting a haircut."

"No. Guess again."

"I hate this game, Jim. What is it?"

"Just got off the phone with Mike Atkinson."

"Who?"

"He's a talent scout. He's the guy that can get you time at the Comedy Store…"

"On Sunset?"

"Yeah."

"How do you know him?" I asked.

"High school. Reconnected through Facebook."

"Wow. My ass is sweating. I didn't even know an ass could sweat."

"Sure, everything can sweat. Skin has holes everywhere. Just relax, though."

"I gotta do well, Jim. Bills are piling up like pastrami, and Meredith wants me to call her brother." I showed him the card.

"Costco," he said. "Oh, God. You know they sell coffins there?"

"Really?"

"Yeah, put my great aunt in one last fall. Nice. 18-gauge steel. Real strong."

"How strong does something need to be in order to sit underground and rot? Anyway, I need to bring home more money. It's not fair to Meredith."

"I'm telling you, once Mike hears your act, he's gonna start bookin' you at bigger clubs—the bigger the club, the bigger the check. Deep breath, deep breath. Just look out for a powerful guy with dark hair and a mustache."

Jim's description of Mike, the talent scout, sounded like that of Hitler: dark hair, mustache, power. How would I identify a man with power? Would he be carrying a sword?

I couldn't really prepare more than I had—my routine had been working pretty well, and I'd been getting consistent laughs. Sure, tonight would've been a good night to try out some new material, but with Hitler on the horizon, maybe that wasn't such a good idea. Part of me wished that Jim would've just crammed another granola bar in his hole and not said a thing.

Barista girl dimmed the lights and patrons clapped, whistled, and woo-hooed as the darkness swallowed more and more of the room. A lady sprinkled something in her coffee, and the man next to her licked the milky froth off of a stirrer. A teenage couple held hands—it was hard to tell if they were boy and girl, or girl and girl, or boy and boy, but they were already laughing at the shape of their bear claw, so I liked them. My armpits started sweating, but this time, I'd sewn tube socks inside my undershirt, or rather, Meredith had. "It's what all the pros do," a guy at another open mic had said.

Jim charged up to the stage from the bathroom, which doubled as our green room, and wiped his hands on his corduroys. He took the mic out of the stand, greeted the clientele and worked through the insecure I-can't-hear-you routine.

"Get a hearing aid," one guy said, his hands cupped around his mouth.

The crowd laughed. So did I.

"It's gonna be fun," Jim said. Everything he said had a high inflection at the end of it, like he was posing a question. "We have a great show for you tonight," he went on. A show? I thought. This is Koffee Korner, Jimbo—you just ran out from the toilet. "We've got music, poetry, and some laughs. Let's get started! Are you guys ready?" My heartbeat picked up and I could feel it in my ears like a metronome. Jim pulled a piece of paper from his pocket. "First, let's welcome Phil and Doug. They'll be performing something from Simon and Garfunkel. Let 'em hear you!"

Phil and Doug started playing "The Only Living Boy in New York." It was a favorite of mine. They didn't know the words and occasionally sang "the only *little* boy in New York."

Jim came over and sat down next to me. He smelled of coconut sunscreen. "Come on," he said, trying to get everyone to clap along. There were only two takers.

Simon and Garfunkel played their last notes and threw their picks into the audience. An ovation ensued. They bowed and walked into the crowd, high-fiving and fist-pounding patrons, and took their seats by the door.

People started gibbering. Barista girl flashed the lights. Jim hopped on stage and raised the mic stand. "Our next performer is gonna read us a poem. Let's give him a warm Koffee Korner welcome!"

The poet sat down on the stool and took a while to get situated. He rolled up his sleeves on his black dress shirt, rubbed his hands on his slacks, and cleared his throat. "Good evening, KK," he whispered. I didn't think it was a good idea to abbreviate Koffee Korner. It put you one "K" away from some serious shit. Jim sat down next to me. The poet stroked his stubble for a few seconds, then commenced:

"A grass stain on my new khakis that Mom just bought,
Being a boy scout made me a big shot.
Cooties were all over girls;
Dad taking me to get a haircut and losing my curls.
Eating my vegetables was always a chore,
Forgetting my homework and so much more..."

"I think *he* should date your daughter," I said.

Jim laughed.

I headed outside to get some separation from the noise, lights, heat, and the bard. Soon it'd be my turn—I visualized myself performing: conversing, slinging jokes, getting applause and saluting the crowd with my glass. My four-minute set would determine my mood for the next four weeks. As scary as it was, though, I loved it: stand-up was without bullshit, without censorship. No airbrushing, no high-fructose corn syrup. No staff meetings, no small talk. You're funny, they laugh; you're not, they don't. Pure, honest, vicious, solitary. The ancient art of storytelling, only with a mic and a spotlight, or, in the case of Koffee Korner, a couple of flashlights held by the barista.

I needed tonight to go well, and not just because of Costco or Mike, but because of me. It'd been two years since I'd moved from Portland, and I'd gotten around, flung jokes ahead of (I told my family and friends that I'd opened for them) Tom Papa and Kathleen Madigan, but my big break had really just been meeting Meredith—a wonderful woman who spent a good amount of her money on me. But certainly Mike and Costco loomed—Mike with his ability to unlock the Sunset Strip, and Costco with its khakis and shiny name tag. I didn't want a name tag. I wanted my face, my work, and my jokes to be my name tag.

A woman was now performing a song on a ukulele. Her fingers

strummed the tight strings, launching happy sounds into the air. I wondered if anything angry had ever been played on ukuleles; I'd always thought of them as guitars that hadn't quite yet gone through puberty.

A nice car, something German, pulled up in front of Koffee Korner. I thought it was Mike. He got out, and I went over the checklist: dark hair, check; mustache, check; power… not sure, but he was carrying a metal briefcase and wearing brown loafers with tassels that bopped as he sauntered. It was sad to see my fate lie in the hands of a man with decorative leather shoes. He entered, and he and Jim hugged by the front door. They patted each other on the back really good, like they were burping each other.

Mike sat near the back and crossed his legs. Jim took the stage as the woman played the last notes of her song. "Beautiful… just beautiful. Next up," he said, "we have a very promising and funny comic. He's a regular here, and a big part of the Koffee Korner family. Please welcome Mister Grayson Matthews!"

The crowds' eyes burned into me as I walked inside and weaved my way through chairs and tables and empty coffee cups that sat on the floor and long legs that lay in repose. The stage was mine. The crowd—if you could call thirty or so people a crowd—was loud. I hugged Jim as he handed me the mic. The barista added another flashlight to her bouquet and rapidly turned them on and off to create a strobe effect. I swallowed hard and took a deep breath.

"Wow, thank you… don't clap that hard—you can't get that back. Give it up for Jim, everybody," I said. The first few moments the crowd always liked you; they cheered for you, took in your face, your mannerisms and wanted you to succeed, but the rest had to be earned. I took a sip of putrid Koffee Korner water. "And just so you know, Jim," I said, "while I appreciate being called a Koffee Korner family member, I don't want to be related to anyone in this place. Kinda like that Olive Garden saying: 'When you're here, you're family.' When was the last time you were at Olive Garden and wanted to be related to any of the 400-pound people going apeshit on breadsticks and minestrone?"

A nice laugh echoed through Koffee Korner. I looked Mike's

way—since he was far in the back it was hard to see him. Most of his figure was dark, except for some of his face that was partially lit by the neon "OPEN" sign, which actually read "OPE"; the "N" had burned out a few months ago, but Jim said he liked it that way, that it sounded sexy and Spanish.

Mike was typing on a laptop. I decided to go after him a little: "Look at this guy... just tappin' away. Doin' a little online shopping, buddy? How's the download of Turbo Tax comin' along?"

Mike laughed. I hadn't done any material from my set, but this was working. A polished comic once advised me not to go through my routine always set on delivering my punchlines, that I might find something more interesting along the way.

"So, folks, I've come here to discuss an important matter, a personal matter. I want to break-up with my girlfriend. I really do. But I can't. And it's not because of any of the things that you'd expect."

"Sex," a fat-faced guy shouted.

"Not even, pal. I told you… not something you'd expect."

"She's cheating on you."

"Relax, buddy—this ain't 21 questions." I looked over at Mike. His head was still angled towards his computer screen. "No, the reason I can't break-up with her is because of all the material she gives me."

Only a single guffaw.

I stared at the bright lights, saw the spots dance across my eyes, and blotted my forehead with my jacket sleeve.

"Seriously, though," I continued, "I've tried to end it, but I'd rather have a failing relationship than have to wait in the unemployment line."

Jim laughed hard—a good steakhouse-style laugh.

"One time we're at the Farmers' Market, and there's this guy with a stand and a sign that says FREE TIBET. My girlfriend asks me about it. I'm figuring that she wants more information on the plight of the Tibetans, but no, she tells me that she's never had any Tibet, and that she'd like to try some—especially for *free*."

The joke sat still. I could feel beads of sweat slither their way down my back.

"And part of me wants to explain it to her, let her really know what's going on. But the comic in me—the guy that needs material—just says, 'Let's see what happens... this should be good.' So we walk over and she asks the guy if she can have some Tibet. I'm not quite sure what she expected Tibet to be—a type of fish? Anyhow, the guy looks at her the way a kid does when he finds out how babies are made.

"Another time, I said I was taking her to Chili's for dinner and she showed up with a backpack, a passport, and a Spanish/English dictionary. They say a sense of humor is the most important thing in a relationship, but they don't specify whether or not the laughs have to be shared."

A soft chuckle. A woman's sneeze. Then a couple God bless you's.

I sat down on the stool. Bill Cosby style. Drank a good gulp of water.

"I'm thinking about marrying her... really am. I could use the job security, especially in this economy. Maybe even go to Chile for the honeymoon."

Mike had ditched the laptop; he now worked with a pen and pad.

"I'm not sure about marriage, though... even the rice that's thrown at weddings kills pigeons."

Nothing. I untangled the mic cord.

"Anyhow, you know it's bad when I'm the smart one in the relationship. In general, women are supposed to be the sharp ones—they get the better test scores, they're skinnier, they live longer. People say: Are we ready for a woman president?—hell yes we are! I mean, haven't we done the 'man' thing, haven't we done it like *44* times?

"And here's proof that women are smarter. What's a woman's best friend?"

The crowd answered: "Diamonds!"

"That's right," I said, "diamonds." I walked the stage a bit. Felt the weight of silence. The same guy that told me not to worry about punchlines, told me that the difference between novices and pros was how they handled the quiet. "Diamonds are precious gems that last a lifetime and can be sold at any time for the same price, even more, and what's a man's best friend? A dog! A furry little bastard that licks his own crotch and dies ten years later."

A nice-sized laugh, one that I desperately needed. I placed the mic back in the stand and shoved my hands deep in my pockets.

"Before I did the relationship thing, though, I was a big friends-with-benefits guy." An older woman said something, and I thought I could take advantage of it. "What was that?" I asked.

"Benefits?" she said. "Like health care?"

Koffee Korner burst into laughter.

"No, no," I said, "not like health care, like sex—without all the other stuff. But let me tell you guys something, it's not as good as it sounds. Friends-with-benefits is a lot like communism: perfect in theory, disastrous in reality. Homes ruined, villages destroyed, dead people all over the place.

There were a lot of "smilers" in this crowd. People that seemed to be laughing on the inside—I hated those types. This happened when the two-drink minimum was replaced with espressos and cupcakes.

"Guess I'm at a strange place in my life—a purgatory of man, if you will—one where I can grow a beard, yet I'm still not sure what a 401K is. It's just a *really* long marathon, right?"

I leaned against the stool, listened to a few giggles.

"Guess there's a time when backpacks become briefcases, bikes become cars, milk becomes wine, and I think I'm still stuck in the middle, unsure of what I want. Maybe I just want to get older without aging, maybe that's why I do this... maybe I think that telling jokes will keep me young forever. Tell you what job I really want: underwear designer... and not for women, but for men. Have you seen what they put on some of the boxers out there? Whales wearing sombreros. Jesus on a skateboard. I always wonder what those board meetings are like: 'Bob, what do you have for us today?' 'Well, so glad you asked, Ted... just came out with a beauty—Gandhi in a racecar.' 'Oh, fantastic, Bob... such creativity from you guys over in graphics.' And don't get me wrong, I love laughing; I love *making* people laugh... just not when I'm undressing."

Mike laughed heartily. It was like when the *Wizard of Oz* changed from black-and-white to color.

"Want to thank you guys for coming out tonight. It's been raining off and on, and I know how L.A. can shut down with just a few drops."

I pulled the mic from the stand.

"I've lived here for a couple years now, and I still think that people are making up freeways. It feels like L.A. has more freeways than the church has saints. People pull me aside all the time and say, 'Okay, buddy, here's what you're gonna do, like it's some Navy Seal operation… you're gonna take the 110 to the 5, the 5 to the 2, the 2 to the 210, and that should get you to where you wanna go… oh, call me if you need me.'"

As the audience laughed, I took another sip of water.

"I don't even know how you guys learn to drive out here; it's like never touching a woman and then being forced to sleep with a porn star."

A strong laugh, one that lingered.

"Do you know that if L.A. were a state it would rank 9th in population? Over 224 languages are spoken here, and only 45 percent of its residents were actually born here. But that's the beauty of this place. We're America's everything pizza."

It was quiet, then the fat-faced guy said, "Someone was on Wikipedia today."

I looked out into the vat of darkness. Faces bobbed like buoys.

"Los Angeles is the only city in the world where you can drive a Korean car to Little Ethiopia to order French food from a transvestite in a Japanese restaurant… and God do I love it."

Chuckles. A few of 'em. I drew a deep breath. I debated whether I should try my new closing. I'd never performed it in front of anyone but my bathroom mirror and Meredith.

"I'll leave you with this, my friends—something we can learn from. Not too long ago I was asked to substitute a kindergarten class. Before you panic, let me tell you that my mom is a kindergarten teacher, and one day she asked me to sub for her. It was legal and everything."

An older couple giggled, then one of them snorted.

"When I entered the class I was confused. I tried slingin' some of my better jokes, but they didn't go for my friends-with-benefits stuff or my L.A. freeway bits, so I switched it up a little—tried a routine of cooties, doodies, and boogers. I'm versatile, people."

A man blew his nose and emitted a foghorn sound.

"On the back wall of the classroom a sign read 'The average kindergartener laughs 400 times a day. The average adult laughs only eight.'

"Eight. Like the amount of cylinders in a Pontiac GTO, like the amount of glasses of water we're supposed to drink daily. Where did our enthusiasm for life go? When did we have to start penciling-in fun? We could all learn something from these five-year-olds."

Mike sat still.

"We could all try to enjoy life's simple pleasures a little more. Of course I wouldn't mind flaring out a guitar solo in front of 60,000 women, but I do have to make peace with the fact that it ain't gonna happen.

"I guess happiness is simple, though.

"Happiness is finding a twenty in your jeans.

"Happiness is a cold beer and the game.

"Happiness is holding your girlfriend's hand… even if she doesn't know what Tibet is."

The crowd laughed politely.

"Thank you, everybody. I'm Grayson Matthews."

I put the mic back in the stand. The applause grew louder. It was over. Jim came running up and gave me a hug.

"Nice job," he said. "Really nice."

"Thanks, Jim."

People patted my back as I stepped down and walked off. That was another thing about open mics—when you were done, you just walked into the crowd; you didn't disappear behind a heavy burgundy curtain. Barista girl smiled at me. I felt strange, moving slowly, like I was underwater.

I headed towards the restroom, like every comic here did after their set. Right after performing, I'd go to the bathroom and lock myself in a stall and listen to what people had to say about me. People were honest when they thought no one was listening. Jim introduced the next act. Another comic. His name was Louie; Louie was half-black, half-Chinese. His first joke was always about how he grew up eating soul food with chopsticks.

In the men's room I claimed the handicapped stall. It was my favorite; it had its own sink and mirror, and was the size of the house I grew up in. I sat down on the toilet and waited, listening to the hum of the air vent and the laughter that penetrated the walls. I folded toilet paper into lousy origami, looked at myself in the mirror, picked at my teeth, plucked an eyebrow hair and smoothed my cowlick. I removed my blazer and dress shirt and placed them on the hook attached to the stall door. My heartbeat slowed and I could feel my face regain its natural, pale color.

A few guys entered. It was hard to decipher much from their shoes apart from the fact that fashion wasn't a concern of theirs—who wore Birkenstocks on a Friday night? What was Birkenstock's slogan? Never talk to women again. They kept quiet, did what they had to do and left.

A couple minutes later, a new guy came in and tried to enter my stall. I panicked.

"Occupied," I answered in an English accent that was more *Chitty Chitty Bang Bang* than Jude Law.

I peeked under the stall door to check his shoes. They were Mike's tassel loafers. He went into the normal-size stall adjacent to mine. Jim soon followed. I didn't have to check his shoes; he announced his arrival.

"Hello there, my friends," he said to the row of urinals.

I sat there. I listened. The sweat socks itched my underarms.

"So, Mike, happy you came?" Jim asked.

"Yeah, thanks for pestering me. Always good to see the young, up-and-coming ones."

Mike flushed. Jim didn't. They went to the sinks, turned on the faucets and pumped the soap dispensers. I focused.

"What'd you think of Gray?" Jim asked.

Yes, what'd you think of Gray?

Mike dried his hands with a couple paper towels. "Well, I know you're big on him, but his stuff seemed a little facile."

Facile? I thought.

"Facile?" Jim said.

"Yeah, he's good in this setting, but he's not quite ready for bigger clubs. His set's disconnected, and his ending was a little too gooey for me. Don't get me wrong, though, he's got something; he handled heckling well, and he's young. Right now, he's doing what's best—putting in the hard miles. I'm just looking for something fresh—not the same old girlfriend-and-relationship stuff."

"He's been working at this for a while now, Mike."

"Trust me; I'm doing him a favor."

"Is he close?" Jim asked.

I felt as though they were talking about a piece of pork: Is he close? Is he ready? Should he be flipped?

"Sure," Mike said, "he's close, but a lot of people go their whole lives at close, a lot of people give up at close. I have to run. Thanks for the invite."

"Yeah, good to see you."

The bathroom door opened and Mike headed out. A minute later, Jim followed.

I bit down on my lip and stared at the ceiling, my eyes in line with a brown patch of something. I could see the conveyor belt at Costco, feel the crinkle of Depends as I scanned their barcodes, hear the beep, beep, beep.

GRAVEYARD SHIFT

* * *

It was a Tuesday night like most others when Luis arrived at The Estates to work the graveyard shift. The security guard before him had forgotten to take down the flag, so Luis headed over. Old Glory was flying at half-staff. Luis wasn't sure why, but with all the horror in the world, it might have just been easier to leave it that way. He uncleated the cord, unclasped the hook, and folded the flag into large triangles. With the flag tucked under his arm, he walked across the dew-soaked grass, back into his booth, and placed it in the wooden box.

The Estates Community that Luis surveyed rested on 159 gated acres. With only one entrance, residents and guests all had to pass by Luis. He wrote the names of those who visited and jotted down their plate numbers, too.

The booth—or Estate House, as residents called it—that Luis worked in was 96 square feet. In it, was a built-in desk, small refrigerator, phone, and half bath. A thirteen-inch TV/VCR combo sat on the floor and the sink in the bathroom dripped every twelve seconds.

Luis reached into his pocket and pulled out his wife's prescription for Coumadin. The bottle had been refilled a couple weeks before her passing, so it was still mostly full. He ran his thumb over the smooth label, across her name, Elba Padilla. He twisted the cap off and poured a few of the pills into his palm. They were circular and yellow and looked like candy. He poured the rest of the Coumadin onto his desk. There were thirty-one pills, and when his shift ended at six in the morning, he would take the early bus over to Rocky Point, sit on his favorite bench, stare at the ocean, and swallow the pills.

A limousine waited for Luis to take note of it. Cigar smoke and cool jazz wafted from the open sunroof. He clicked a button and the iron gate opened. Another person entered a few minutes later. This one drove a red sports car and never turned off his high beams. Luis shielded his eyes, but the driver ignored the hint.

Elba had passed seven months ago. Seven months ago next Wednesday, Luis thought. He couldn't believe how slowly time had passed. Whenever someone asked him about his wife and how he was doing with it all, he said, "If you want to live forever, have your wife die." He was closer to her now than he was when she was living, though. Life brought so many complications, but when someone passed, the memories of strife seemed to occupy the casket, too, and Luis never replayed the sad moments, the bad times; instead, he saw her rubbing lotion on her elbows before bed, working masa into corn husks around Christmastime, and heard her singing "Tres Dias" as she plucked dandelions in the backyard.

Luis wondered if he would go quickly. He'd gone to his local library a couple times—early in the morning a few minutes after it had opened so that no one would be at the computer terminal—and searched about Coumadin overdoses. There was a site that detailed what happened to the body, how the blood-thinner basically induced a heavy amount of internal bleeding.

He figured people wouldn't be surprised. "Who? Oh, that guy," they'd say. "The old man. Yeah, he always seemed lonely to me. How'd he do it?" they'd ask. Everyone always wanted to know how it was done, like there was something telling about that.

Some time later, Luis went to the bathroom and sat on the foam toilet seat. When using the john, a sign had to be placed in the window of the booth, notifying the Community that the guard was using the toilet.

It read: SORRY I'M USING THE RESTROOM. BACK IN A JIFFY! ☺

A while back, he'd gone ahead and covered some of the words with electrical tape, so it now read: ~~SORRY I'M~~ USING THE RESTROOM. ~~BACK IN A JIFFY! ☺~~

After returning to the desk, he flipped through the guest log and filled in some dates. He then fixed his eyes on the road perpendicular to his booth. There wasn't any traffic, as it was a Tuesday in a bedroom community, but every now and then, a car rushed by and he wondered if the driver had spent a night worth remembering.

This hour of the night led to nostalgia attacks, and Luis would call his home from the booth and listen to Elba's voice on the message machine. He'd savor the recording, hang up, and sometimes call again. Luis had been out with a couple women since her death, women he'd met at bars, mostly. But it was hard to love after death. He thought love was limited, and that he'd used up all of his.

He pulled out his Thermos and drank. The coffee cascaded down his throat and warmed him. He opened the paper, flipped to the "Calendar" section of the *Times*, and read his horoscope.

SCORPIO: Today you will feel the power of seduction and the pull of the present. You'll experience a wizbang of life. Tonight: hang out with loved ones.

Then he read Elba's.

ARIES: An ingenious idea could fall flat. Let go, and let others find a different solution. Tonight: A must appearance.

Was it time that pulled us apart... or was it just us? he thought. Did I answer a question wrong one day or simply not ask the right one? And then, after that, did I make a habit of it? Maybe it's just love's evolution... maybe what starts as kisses and drive-ins ends with quiet and prayers.

Still though, Luis often regretted the little things, like not saying "please" more, not squeezing her hand while driving, and not remembering to turn on her half of the heating blanket so she could've always crawled into warm sheets.

The cup of coffee on the desk steamed and killed the scent of mildew in the booth. He stared out the window onto the boulevard, then gazed at the sky. Shy stars hung under a yellow moon. He savored the bitter taste of coffee and the sight of the night sky. He felt powerful knowing when and how he'd go. He didn't have any children, and only a few friends. Everyone would be able to take one car to his funeral.

A car raced by on the main road, its engine humming, its pipes growling. Luis tracked its lights until it left his gaze.

A few seconds later, there was a crash. The noise was sudden and ripped apart the quiet like a crack of thunder. It fell still once again.

Luis jumped to his feet, thinking it must have been the car that just sped by. Many nights, he studied the main road in hopes that he'd see someone pop a tire, catch a glimpse of a coyote in search of food, or help a lost driver find the freeway, but nothing had ever happened.

He darted from the booth, clumsily, and pushed towards the main road. Mist hung heavy and the droplets found his face as he ran. In this sleepy seaside town, the residents insisted that no streetlights be put up, so the dark was blacker than usual. Luis struggled. His legs burned and sweat pushed out his pores. It'd been so long since he'd felt his heart beat strongly. He pressed on, his thighs prickling, his breath heavy. He thought that maybe lights would be flashing up ahead, that maybe someone had already pulled over, but he couldn't spot a thing. After continuing a bit more, he heard the sound of an idling engine and picked up on the pungent odor of burnt rubber and noticed the glow of brake lights down in a thicket of tall brush.

Luis rushed down into the weeds, where foxtails and burrs dug into his pants. Glass cracked under his boots. "Hello? Are you all right?" he said, trying to open the driver's-side door. He wanted to call 9-1-1, but he had forgotten his cell phone in his bag. Quickly, he darted around to the other side of the car and attempted to yank open the passenger-side door. It took a while, but Luis eventually got it open. The cabin light cut on and he saw the driver: a young woman with coffee-colored skin. Her head was cocked to the side and obscured by a deflated airbag. Luis pushed the bag down, and inspected her scraped cheeks and bleeding forehead. He didn't know whether or not to touch her, but decided he might hurt her more by trying to move her, and he didn't think he had the strength to do so, anyway. "Hello?" he said again. Her chest wasn't rising or sinking. "Please, sweetie. Talk to me. Can you hear me?"

In the backseat, Luis spotted the woman's purse. Inside, he found her cell phone and called 9-1-1. The call went through quickly. "9-1-1," the man said. "What's your emergency?"

"An accident," Luis said. His breath was heavy. "A car accident on Crest Road. A young woman. She doesn't look as though she's breathing, and she's got a big gash on her forehead."

"Okay, sir," the man said. "Help is on the way. Can you tell me, if you can, where on Crest?"

"Uh, not far from Highridge, down a ways, off the road," Luis said. He ran his hand over the woman's shoulder.

"Is there danger of the car blowing up? Any smoke or signs of fire?"

"No," Luis said.

"Do you know CPR, sir?"

"No."

"Are you able to assist in other capacities?"

"I'm old and don't know what to do," Luis said.

"I'll help you. She needs you, sir."

"Okay, yes."

The 9-1-1 operator gave Luis various instructions. He didn't want Luis to move the woman, but he did want him to try and find a pulse. Luis placed the phone on the dash while tending to the woman. He lifted the sleeve of her shirt and placed his thumb on her wrist, over a small tattoo of a strawberry. Then he lowered his lips to the woman's heavily pierced ears. "I'm here," he said. "Can you hear me?"

"Anything?" the operator said.

Luis picked up the phone. "No."

"Place your hand over her heart; it can be easier to pick up sometimes."

"Her forehead is still bleeding," Luis said.

"Get her heartbeat first," the man said.

Luis did as he was told and slid his hand underneath the woman's blouse and against her smooth skin. Even though it was cold outside, her skin was warm. The woman's pulse was slow, with seconds between beats.

"Anything?" the operator asked.

"It's tired, but there."

"Good," he said. "The ambulance should be there soon. You'll hear the sirens. Keep listening to me… now try to get that gash on her head to stop bleeding."

A sweater was coiled on the backseat floor, and Luis scooped it up and pressed it against the woman's forehead. Blood saturated the fabric and, in time, the bleeding stopped. He then tucked a few strands of black hair behind her ear. Her perfume smelled strongly of cinnamon. "Are you there?" he said directly into her ear, feeling his warm breath ricochet against his mouth.

"Sir," the operator said. "Do you hear the ambulance?"

He ran his fingers over the woman's neck. "You're gonna be okay," he said.

"Sir. Are you there, sir?"

"Yes, yes."

"Is her heart still beating?"

Again, Luis placed his hand atop the woman's chest. Her skin wasn't as warm as before. "Yes, barely," he said.

"Do you see a purse around?" the man asked. "Any place where she might keep her ID."

Luis plucked out her wallet and opened it. He squinted to read the information. "It's a Nevada ID," he said. "Her name's Anaya Cooper." He removed the license from its plastic slot and called out the ID number. Underneath her ID was a photo of her and a young man. The two of them sat at opposite ends of a small table and leaned towards the center like eaves.

In the distance, the whine of sirens cut through the night. Luis took Anaya's hands and worked his thumbs across her palms.

He figured people would be surprised. "Who? Oh, that guy," they'd say. "The old man. The weird-looking guy. What'd he do?" they'd ask. He closed his eyes and slowed his breath.

The ambulance pulled up. The air brakes hissed.

Bright lights flooded the scene and flashed across the insides of Luis's eyelids. He moved aside and watched strong men in dark uniforms pull Anaya from the car, secure her to a gurney, and lift her steadily through the tall grass. The doors on the back of the ambulance swung open and the legs of the stretcher collapsed as Anaya was slid into place. She was strapped down in the back and the paramedics began working on her immediately, cutting off her clothes and fitting her face with an oxygen mask. The truck's engine rumbled and grunted, and the heat from the muffler mixed with the cold air and formed plumes of smoke.

Luis didn't know why, but as the truck's doors slammed shut

and the ambulance lurched forward, he raised his arm as if waving good-bye. I wish I'd been better, he thought. He pulled in a few deep breaths of night air and tracked the ambulance for as long as he could, until the sirens' screams were quiet and the truck's taillights became little red dots in the distance. Then he brought his arm back down.

BIRDS OF PARADISE

* * *

Today's Thanksgiving. I'm back in town, visiting my folks for the first time in maybe eight, nine years. All I know is that a new president's in charge and I've had to renew my passport, so, yeah, it's been a while.

My flight touched down about an hour ago, and I'm driving a rental, a blue Mustang convertible. It's not warm, but I put the top down anyway. The previous renter programmed all the presets to mariachi stations. The accordions and trumpets and *ay ay ays* don't scream Pilgrims or Indians, which is why I don't change a thing.

Driving the car feels liberating. I get off the freeway and take side streets. I'm on Crenshaw, heading north. Chinese restaurants, supermarkets, churches, bus stops, and gas stations flank the street. As I near Whiffletree Lane, I think of Cole, the man who encouraged me to get away, the man who freed me.

My mother's told me that the bird and trimmings will be served at three. It's only two, and I don't need the extra hour with my parents, so I pull down Whiffletree Lane. The street's bowered by oaks of all the same size; it's as though the trees had a meeting and said, "Let's all grow like this, with our branches fanning out like menorahs."

I park in front of his brick house. The driveway is empty. The leaves rustle; the wind whines.

After a few deep breaths, I inspect my teeth in the rearview mirror—they're crumb free. I smooth my thinning hair and cup one of my hands around my mouth and exhale. My breath's subpar, so I pop in a mint.

As I walk to the door, I notice the grass isn't as green as it used to be, and that some of his flowers, his favorite ones—birds of paradise, I think they're called—are dying.

How long's it been? Too long. I was a confused twenty-something with a tight jaw, long lashes, and creamy skin. We never slept together because I wasn't ready, but I've never felt closer to anyone else.

I ring the bell. I'm nervous, scared he won't recognize me. Age has picked on me with expression lines and dark bags that hang under my eyes like hammocks.

There are some sounds coming from behind the door: the creaking of wood, the shuffle of feet. The latch is unfastened; the door is pulled open slowly.

"Cole," I say as he continues to open the door. "It's me— "

"I know that voice," he says softly. "Gregory."

He's not the same man. He's standing there, in the doorway, leaning against the frame in stained, navy sweat pants. He doesn't have a shirt on and his shoulders, his what-used-to-be 44-regular shoulders are tired. The thick black chest hair I used to run my hands through is gray and thin, and the medallions that used to rest in the center of it are dull. His ribs are exposed and his arms are no thicker than his wrists. With his face angled at the brick, he says something.

"What?" I say.

"Aids," he says. "A couple years back."

I want to say something, but I don't. I can never seem to find the right words when it matters. Instead, I just reach over and grab his hand. I hold it. What once was a thick man's hand, is now brittle. His knuckles are bumpy as challah bread and his veins are plump and squishy.

"I always hoped you'd come back and ring this bell," he says, and I can tell the sentence takes a lot out of him. "Come in."

Inside, everything is as it was—the oriental rugs are rich and red and feel plush under my feet. The couches are brown and as weathered as he is. His baby grand's in the corner, and I can see myself sitting on the couch next to it, writing term papers, asking him for help.

He leads me into his bedroom. I drag my left hand along the curves of his sleigh bed, and help him in. He lies down and howls till he hasn't any air in his chest. I sit in a recliner, off to the side. The TV's in the corner and the mute icon dances across the screen. A cooking show's on and a chef chops scallions and flashes a big smile while doing so.

He struggles with the sheets, so I hop up and help him out.

"How long's it been?" he asks.

"Too long," I say.

"You look good," he says.

"Your eyes are closed," I say.

"I think of you often," he says.

"Me too," I say. "Never met another like you. Not even close."

"Will you stay awhile?" he says, removing his hand from the covers and searching for mine.

HIT AND STAY

* * *

Penn continued to drive through the night. Snow and gales of wind assailed his SUV as he barreled towards home, his foot steady on the gas, his hands positioned firmly at ten and two. Heat billowed from the vents on the dashboard and moved loose strands of hair on his face. He didn't want to replay the scenario—the quiet L.A. hotel room, the closed drapes, the underwear on the floor, the moaning, the taste of her lips—but the SUV's quiet cabin was a hotbed for reflection.

His headlights brushed a green highway sign, indicating that there were eighty-nine miles left on his journey home to Lake Tahoe. With the winter weather, it might take Penn more than two hours, but that was all right. How would he look at Kimberly after what he'd done?

"Don't marry young," people had told him a few years ago when he'd passed around the idea of proposing. "You haven't tested the waters." Cliché after cliché came at him, and while the marriage advice was stale and up there with "enjoy each day like it's your last" and "don't let anyone tell you something's impossible," it wasn't amiss.

Becky had been with the company for a couple months now; there'd been some mild flirting, but Penn just thought that was the way she was, and he flirted back from time to time, knowing that it was just a game. Becky saw the wedding band on his finger; she could put two and two together.

But on this recent trip, Penn and Becky had found themselves at the hotel bar, overlooking the glimmering L.A skyline. There was a meeting early in the morning, and most of the company's employees had gone to bed. She approached Penn and slid onto the chair next to his. They drank, and their eyes held one another in the empty bar. The piano man played his versions of "So What" and "Stardust," songs that made people more attractive and made conversations more interesting. The right strap of Becky's blue dress kept slipping off her freckled shoulder, and she left her smooth skin exposed longer than normal before bringing the strap back up. Her breasts were pressed up and together, and when she crossed her legs, one of her black heels dangled a few inches from her foot, making it seem as though she was already undressing. Penn remembered the way she reached over and touched his right hand.

The worst part was that Penn had only slept with Becky because of the confidence Kimberly had given him. Many times she'd reaffirmed his self-esteem, telling him he was worthy of love, that he was better-looking than he imagined, and that he deserved the best.

Penn believed the burden would be lightened if he told Kimberly, but at the same time, he thought the words might destroy her, and that's not what he wanted. It'd taken cheating for him to know how much he loved her, but who would believe a line like that?

The tapping of a snare drum leaked out from the speakers, accompanied by the beat of an upright bass and the trill of a clarinet. He lowered the window and let the cold air flow into the sweltering cabin.

Was there a perfect scenario? Penn thought. He let his mind wander. When he got home maybe Kimberly would be crying.

What's wrong? Penn would say.

I did something terrible, Kimberly would answer.

Kimberly would go on to tell Penn that she'd slept with someone else, that she was sorry, and that it didn't mean anything. After that, he'd say the same thing. Two wrongs, one right. But even thinking about her sleeping with someone else made him sick. That wasn't at all what he wanted.

High school sweethearts turned lovers turned husband and wife turned roommates—that's what they were. Penn found it more and more difficult to make her laugh. Where there'd been kisses, there were now smiles. Where there'd been heat, there was now platitude. Where there'd been love, there was now familiarity.

Was it dumb to think that a transgression could put the marriage back on the right track? Sure, they'd tied the knot, but maybe this could double-knot it. In Kimberly's third grade classroom there was a poster that she'd had Penn hang up this past August: Mistakes are Opportunities for Learning. Maybe, he thought. Maybe. Sometimes all there was in life was maybe.

The highway patrol was out and directing traffic into a single lane; there'd been an accident on the freeway. Noticing that his gas gauge was nearing empty, Penn broke away from the pack and took to a gas station.

When the tank was full, Penn climbed back into the heated cabin, turned the key, and pressed the pedal. Snow drifted towards the windshield like little stars falling from the sky. The wipers took care of the weather with quick swipes, and seeing that, Penn couldn't help but think that it would be nice to have something similar when it came to emotions, something that could clean and restore balance with a flick. In reality, when things got dirty, all people could do was try to find a new vantage point and do their best to look through the filth.

As Penn drove towards the onramp, he noticed the red glow of brake lights. He stayed to the side, the car idling, the radio playing. He decided to take the back roads. From the glove box, Penn removed a map and found where he was. There was a main road a few miles away, and while a tad tortuous, there wouldn't be any traffic.

As he drove the streets, his headlights illuminated thick pines that wore globs of snow. The yellow lines that divided the two lanes blended together as Penn increased his speed. Sounds of humming tires and brash wind blasted his ears, and when Penn focused on the gusts, they almost seemed to speak to him. Shhhh, he heard them say. Shhhh.

The white road had no defining characteristics, just trees and snow, black everywhere but where the lights hit. Penn drove for an hour and never once saw a car. He wondered what would happen if he were to fall asleep at the wheel and slam into the snowy pines and die on impact. When would he be found? What would Kimberly do when she heard the news? What would she say at his funeral? He pictured his headstone, saw his name carved, the date of his birth, the date of his death and the little hyphen in between. That's what life was signified by—a hyphen. Everything a person did or didn't do contained in a little line, a dash, a minus sign.

Coming around a turn, indications of civilization began to appear in the cones of Penn's headlights. Houses that looked like the kind children drew—with two windows and a door between them and a chimney spouting smoke—began to pop up on both sides of the street. The setting reminded him of Lake Forest, Illinois, where he'd first met Kimberly. He remembered her pale skin, her long fingers, the scar on her chin from a car accident, and her freshly pierced ear lobes, which wore little bandages. Both of their parents had recently divorced, and the two of them talked about what they were going through. Kimberly was handling it better than Penn. He recalled the way he looked then, facial hair sprouting in strange formations, clusters of pimples that looked like Braille riding his forehead. At that time, he'd wanted nothing more than to change the world. Now all he wanted to do was live in it. Kimberly had changed, too. Since the death of her mother a couple of years ago she'd become more distant, sleeping with her eyes facing the wall instead of looking at Penn like she used to. She'd also developed little lines that bookended her mouth like parentheses and made her always look sad.

As he approached a four-way stop, he gazed at a house, the only one that still had its lights on. Inside, an older couple read by the fireplace. They didn't seem to be talking. They didn't move. They just read. They were just there. How did people get to that point?

Penn wondered if the old man had a clear conscience or if he'd just learned how to live with a dirty one. With the pedal pushed down and one eye on the rearview mirror, he watched plumes of smoke exit the elderly couple's brick chimney. The windshield was beginning to fog up, so Penn twisted the dials and allowed the defroster to blow its seductive air over the glass.

When he brought his eyes back up, he noticed something brown, white and low to the ground. It darted into the shafts of his headlights. He punched the brakes and the tires screamed. But he couldn't slow down in time. He tightened his body and closed his eyes. The tires thumped twice as they crushed the animal.

Penn's breathing picked up and his hands began to tremble. He looked in the rearview mirror where his brake lights colored the snow red, but they weren't strong enough to spotlight the damage he'd done. With his eyes closed, he listened to the weather, his car, and his heartbeat. He could feel his arteries expand and contract in his wrists and a persistent pulsing in his neck.

Under the weak moonlight, Penn got out of his vehicle and walked towards the animal, his gaze narrowed so as not to see the horror in its entirety. He had hit and killed a beagle. The legs of the dog were snapped and twisted, and bits of clean white bone pushed through bloodied fur. The dog's eyes were closed as though it had braced itself for impact. Penn brought his hands from the warmth of his coat, placed them on the dog's flank and brushed off the ice and snow that had adhered to its body.

I'm sorry, Penn said. White smoke left Penn's mouth with each syllable. I'm sorry, Penn said again, his hands moving over the dog's coat, rubbing the hide as though a few caresses would resuscitate its limbs and lungs and heart. He searched for an ID tag to identify the dog's owner, but the neck was bare, the dog's name unknown.

He worked his hands under the dog's frame and peeled it from the road. The beagle was heavy and limp in Penn's arms. Its snout hung over the crux of his elbow and bobbed with each step, while the tail moved gently from side to side and made Penn think of a time when the dog was alive.

He placed the dog on the side of the road atop a thick bank of snow that was quickly stained with seeping blood. He turned and looked at the spot where the dog had been hit; there, the blood had already frozen.

Penn crossed into the headlights to examine the front of his car. Blood speckled a cracked bumper, but everything else was fine. Back in the cabin, Penn's breaths rattled from his lips, and his hands were numb and red from the cold. He turned the key and drove, inspecting the peripheries of the white road, expecting another dog to dart in front of his SUV.

The heater blew, but Penn continued to shake. Goosebumps dotted his forearms and ice melted in his boots. Penn pictured the dog's face. He hoped it hadn't suffered. He drove for miles, shivering, blowing on his hands and rubbing his shoulders, but he couldn't warm up.

Things began to look familiar. Penn entered a town that wasn't far from his, where large trees on both sides of the road grew towards one another and permitted little moonlight to slice through. He waited at an intersection and watched a stoplight get pummeled by the wind.

After a few more miles, Penn clicked his blinker and turned right onto his street, a wide boulevard with room to park five or six cars side by side. He drove in the middle, avoiding the snow and debris that had been pushed to the sides by the snow plow. He wondered if Kimberly would be able to tell, if she'd notice the sputter in his speech, the scent on his body, the betrayal on his breath.

It was 11:30. Penn thought Kimberly might be asleep—this was about her bedtime, but the two top dormer windows were bright, giving the façade of the house a pair of yellowish eyes. He pulled up to the garage, killed the headlights, and brought the gear shift up. He lay his head on the steering wheel and felt the rhythm of his heartbeat. His heart had been through it all—the first kiss with Kimberly, the dance at their wedding, the handshake with his father-in-law, the honeymoon, the death of Kimberly's mother, the time in the L.A. hotel room with Becky, the killing of the dog.

He unclipped his seatbelt and walked across the snow. He peered through a window before entering, scared to open the back door of his own house, feeling like an intruder.

Kimberly was sitting on the couch in front of the fireplace, dunking a tea bag in and out of a cup of hot water. The fire's flames were large, the tips blue, and they danced around as gusts of wind found their way down the chimney. Kimberly continued steeping her tea in the scalding water before placing her cup on a nearby table. She closed her eyes and sank into the cushions. Since her hair wasn't pulled back, the strands cascaded over her face like curtains. Penn stuttered through a few more breaths and thought of how cozy and warm it seemed inside, free of his deception. He brought his hand to the cold steel and turned the knob.

The door creaked and Kimberly turned her head. I didn't hear you pull in, she said. How was the conference?

Penn swallowed, took a few steps towards her and tried to speak, but she cut in.

Jesus, she said. You've got blood all over you! She rushed to Penn. Are you bleeding?

Penn looked down at his blood-saturated coat and then at his red-stained fingers. I hit a dog on the way home, he said. I hit and killed a dog.

Oh, God, she said, tucking her hair behind her ears. She helped Penn remove his coat and sweater, and then led him to the couch where she'd been sitting.

It's all my fault, Penn said, struggling to inhale.

Kimberly sat down next to him and ran her hand over his back.

I didn't mean to, he said.

Did you tell the owner? she asked.

Couldn't, he said.

It's been so long since I've seen you like this, she said.

The wood popped and clusters of sparks flew up the chimney. Kimberly grabbed her tea and blew across its surface, then rubbed the nape of Penn's neck.

How did it happen? she asked.

I just took my eyes off the road, he said, placing his hands on her leg.

The fire continued to burn, and Penn studied the way the flickers lit up Kimberly's face. The scar on her chin was showcased in the soft lighting—the difference in texture was noticeable. They sat on the couch, side by side in the warm room, hands intertwined, listening to the rhythm of their breaths, watching the clean snow fall.

DO YOU SEE THE BIG DIPPER?

* * *

Jack and Polly sat on the sloping lawn, bowered by oaks, ready for the outdoor concert to begin. Around them, on blankets of their own, rested other couples, some with children, some elderly, some teenage. People sifted through picnic baskets, and pulled out pasta salad, barbeque chicken, deviled eggs, and large triangular slices of watermelon. Jack lay down on the blanket and aligned his eyes with the tops of the trees. The sun was beginning its descent, as it was seven o'clock in the evening, and Jack studied the way some of the rays trickled through the leaves and cast bright patches along the grass.

"It smells like summer," Jack said. "I have no idea what that means, but it does, doesn't it?"

Polly laughed. "I know what you mean," she said, her hand finding Jack's atop the red plaid blanket.

Jack always loved holding Polly's hands—they were small and soft and fit nicely inside his. Tonight, she'd painted her nails a purple color. "Aubergine," she said it was. Jack thought that was what Europeans called eggplant, but he didn't say that to her. He just continued to listen to the wind play with the trees, and feel the breeze sweep through, and allow for a few leaves to flutter to the ground, a sort of summertime snow.

"Who's playing tonight?" she asked.

"Sax and the City," Jack said, "you know, like last summer. I remembered how much you liked them."

Polly squeezed Jack's hand. "That's so sweet," she said.

The four members of Sax and the City took the stage. The drummer and sax player tinkered with the amps, while the bassist and guitarist fiddled with their strings.

"Weren't there five before?" Polly said. "What happened to the piano player? He was cute. And, *oh my God*, the sax player put on a lot of weight."

"That's the same guy?" Jack said. "Maybe he ate the piano

player." Jack slipped his free hand into the pocket of his khakis and brushed the velvet fibers of the little black box. He thought about a day down the road—maybe he and Polly would be getting ready for a night out with some friends. Polly would be in the bathroom and he'd be looking for his dressy watch and come across this box. He'd remember petting the fibers on this very night; he'd remember thinking how nervous he was, how he swept through the grocery store with a big list, how he bought the perfect blanket, and how the saxophonist had put on a whole bunch of weight. He wanted to remember everything, though—the way the trees looked, what they ate, the songs that were played, and the stars in the sky.

"Doesn't it look dressed up?" Jack overheard an old woman say to what he thought was her husband.

"Doesn't what looked dressed up?" the old man said.

"The sax," she said, "it looks so dressed up—like it's going out or something."

"Marie, you tickle me pink," the old man said.

Jack played with the box, cracked it open, and slid a finger inside to make sure it was still there. It was hard for him to believe. After all, he'd made fun of people who got married, saying they were all co-dependent, that the whole institution was out-of-touch, and that it was just invented so that the government could keep tabs on you. The idea of registering for gifts and having round balls of butter on little plates at the reception used to make him sick to his stomach. Plus, he'd seen his parents. They'd taught him a great deal, mostly what not to do, but still. Some might call it premature—ten months—but he knew. What was the point of waiting when you knew? He'd known since their first encounter at LAX. There was this woman who looked like she'd spent the afternoon in the tub, then lacquered herself with moisturizer, shimmied into tight black jeans and a leather jacket, and wrapped a string of pearls around her neck—a straight proud neck, the most pearly thing about her, pearlier even than the pearls themselves. Who wore pearls with a leather jacket? he thought, figuring her to a harmonious blend of Joan Jett and Audrey Hepburn. She was waiting at the same gate as Jack, D7, passing time, with her legs crossed. Jack wanted to sit close enough to her so that he'd be part of her aura, but not close enough to be in her space. He plopped down with a seat in between them and set his coat in the middle, then opened the paper. Wanting to look smart and impressive, he read the "Calendar" section with "Business" close behind—in case she was one of those. When Polly turned his way, he smiled a light smile, one where his lips curved upwards but didn't part to expose his teeth. "Are you going to read the 'Sports' page?" she asked. "Wanted to see how Kemp did last night—he's having a great year." Jack nodded. Quickly and efficiently, Polly quartered the *Times*. "I'm Jack," he said. "Polly," she answered.

"All right," the saxophonist said. There was a V-shaped sweat stain on the collar of his orange t-shirt. "Who's ready to boogie?"

People clapped. Jack looked at the family to his left, a family of four—a mother, a father, a boy, and a baby girl. The mother's hair was curly and loose, and her jeans were genuinely tattered; she hadn't bought them that way like so many Angelenos. The father wore a cap, and his boy had a sunburn on his nose that was beginning to peel and clutched an action figure—a Roman-style gladiator with two swords crisscrossed over his head. The baby girl was sleeping a deep sleep and not wearing any shoes. They looked happily disorganized. To Jack's right were a couple of teenagers. They both wore the same type of Converse sneakers, sat on a single beach towel, and ate from take-out containers with plastic forks. Tomato sauce slathered the guy's lips.

Polly peeked into the picnic basket that Jack had prepared. He'd ensured that there were two of everything—a Noah's Ark of picnicking—except for champagne; he'd only bought one bottle of that, but he'd picked one with a French name that was difficult to pronounce, one that looked north of forty dollars on appearance alone.

The music started. The drummer brushed the cymbals and the bassist walked his fingers across the strings. Then, moments later, the guitarist added more rhythm. Polly and Jack listened to the steady beat and waited for the sax to come rolling through. Jack didn't know much about jazz, except for the fact that he felt better-looking and more intelligent when it lingered in the air.

He plucked the champagne from the picnic basket; the bottle was cold and icy and made his hands turn white. He took off the foil, unscrewed the wire cage, held the cork, and rotated the bottle. The old man looked over at Jack and smiled, so did the father with the family. Jack poured Polly a glass.

"To us," Jack said.

"To us," Polly said.

But just as Jack was about to bring out the box, the father with the family tapped him on the shoulder and said, "You're making every guy here look terrible," then laughed.

"Leave him alone," the mother said. "You could learn a thing or two."

Jack smiled and stared at the man's chin. It was one of those dimple chins, like John Travolta's. The little boy nestled himself in his father's lap and slid his action figure into the front pocket of his dad's t-shirt.

It's okay, Jack said to himself. So much time to go. It's early, real early. Have some more champagne. Get loose. Let Sax and City work through their playlist. It's only song one.

Polly pulled out her Greek salad; Jack did the same. They clinked cups of dressing and drizzled them on. Jack listened to the cold notes escape the sax's bell and savored the way the sultry music swept through the warm night. He knew that Polly was the right woman for him, because when he was with her, he never wanted to be anywhere else. At work, he dreamed of being at ball games, and sometimes with friends, he wished he were alone, but with Polly, he was always content, stupidly and foolishly content.

"What a cute kid," Jack whispered to Polly, referring to the boy in the father's lap.

"You always say that," Polly said as the saxophonist wailed.

"It's true, though. Hard to find a kid that isn't cute, right? They're like puppies. Even the not-so-cute ones are cute."

"They're so not like puppies," Polly said, tilting back her champagne. "Kids are a whole different thing."

"Of course, of course."

Jack and Polly laughed more, set their champagne glasses

atop the picnic basket and watched the little bubbles in the gold liquid head north and burst.

When the sax player picked up a clarinet, the old man was startled. "What in the world?" he shouted. "How did that happen?"

"Louie, it's a clarinet. He picked up a clarinet," the old woman said.

"Oh," he said. "Thought my hearing aid was acting up again."

Polly squeezed Jack's hand.

The saxophonist, or clarinetist, rocked back and forth. The little boy, comfy in his father's lap, began to clap, copying other audience members. The old man whistled a little to show his appreciation, yet soon after, sneezed, prompting his wife to say, "Louie, you shouldn't whistle so hard. You're gonna blow something out."

"Please, Marie—it's got nothing to do with it. One of these damn crackers went down the wrong pipe. I told you to buy crackers with rounded corners. Why do they need to make the edges so sharp?"

Jack rested his eyes on the old couple's hands; their fingers were so swollen it'd be impossible to remove their wedding rings. Jack then looked over at the teenagers. They didn't talk much, but they laughed a lot. On the rubber toes of the guy's Converse high-tops, scrawled in black marker, was "RC loves CB," and on her shoe was "CB loves RC," but the shoes were new, no more than a couple days out of the box. The little boy played with the drawstrings of his father's hoodie—braiding, tangling, pulling, and tying them. When the boy saw that Jack was looking at him, he stopped, then continued when he understood that Jack didn't seem to care. Another song came to a close, and Jack clapped. The boy did the same, even screamed a little. His mother looked over at Jack and said, "Sorry."

"Kind of ridiculous," Polly leaned over and whispered to Jack.

"What's that?"

"Bringing a little kid and baby to an outdoor concert, I mean—they aren't going to appreciate this."

"Oh, it's kind of nice," Jack said. "More champagne?"

"Yes," Polly said.

They continued to eat their salads, smile between bites, and enjoy the concert. The sun began to set, casting long stripes of red, pink, and yellow across the horizon. Jack liked the way the warm colors of dusk lit Polly's face, giving her skin an inviting glow. Sometimes, many times, actually, Jack found himself staring at her for sheer enjoyment. He imagined it was the way others must have felt when perusing an art gallery. Every feature was where it was supposed to be. He studied the little curve between her nose and top lip. He wanted to shrink himself and lie down in there, curled up like a seed. He looked at her eyelashes—fanned out and dense like a peacock's tail. He took in her eyebrows—immaculately groomed, resembling small, mown hills, too arched, not at their best tonight, but still. He thought of the way she donated twenty percent of her salary to the poor, cared for her sick grandmother, and planned to work as an environmental lawyer so that she could protect endangered species. Just then, he thought he should work that into his popping of the question—add something about how *she* was an endangered species. Or maybe he was, maybe it was *he* who was about to disappear, without her, he would say. But, a few seconds later, he vetoed that idea.

"I'm so happy to be with you tonight." Jack placed his hand on Polly's leg. "In fact, I've been happy with you for a long time."

"I've been happy for a long time, too," Polly said, a piece of arugula caught between her shiny teeth.

Jack thought this might be the perfect time to propose, but he pictured the scene after the answer. People would clap and tap their glasses with their spoons or keys or whatever, and the kid would scream, and the mother would apologize. Polly would explode into a smile. He didn't want her to be embarrassed by a piece of arugula, so he told her about it. "There," Jack said. "Right there."

"Here?"

"No. *There*."

"Is it gone?"

"No... lower."

"Did I get it?"

"No... higher."

"Now?"

"No... to the right... no, *your* right."

"Did I get it?"

"I hate this game," Jack said, leaning in and working it free.

Polly smiled.

Okay, Jack thought, time to relax, re-strategize.

The old couple hummed along with a tune. The teenagers whispered things into each other's ears and giggled every so often, and the family with the little boy and baby girl ate sandwiches. While bad at telling kids' ages, Jack suspected the boy to be about six, as he was clumsy, ate with his fingers, and spoke with his mouth full. The boy's right foot wiggled and he frequently kicked his father by accident, though he did say "sorry" when it happened. The action figure now stood tall between the sodas and wadded-up napkins and, when not eating, the boy would work him around the cans and juice boxes. He was laden with armor and the scowl on his face looked menacing, as if nothing in the poor, weather-beaten fighter's life had ever turned out.

With Polly digging though the picnic basket, Jack scanned the surroundings, discreetly pulled out the box and opened it. He blew hot breath across the diamond and shined it with his sleeve. It sat there, perky, deep amid velvet. The old man saw him and opened his eyes big and wide and winked. Jack slipped the box back into his pocket.

Should I full-name her? Jack thought. Is it too cliché? Isn't love about clichés, though? Polly Elizabeth West? Maybe just Polly West. Should I genuflect? Not genuflect... get down on one knee... genuflecting is a church thing... and I'm already on the ground. The action figure would genuflect, though, swords in hand. He wouldn't be afraid of the concert; he wouldn't care about the music or the perfect time. He would stand up and just say something regal and beautiful: "Milady," he might say, "will thoust give me thy dear hand in matrimony? I, your loving man, promise you a lifetime of serenity and happiness."

"This song is called 'Sonny.' It's one of our favorites," the saxophonist bellowed into the mic. "Everybody having fun so far? I can smell lot of good food—are those ribs?" he said, pointing to the front row. "Uh, one-two," he said. The drummer struck the cymbal; the guitarist readjusted his strap and the bassist twirled his instrument. The saxophonist tapped his foot and waited to join in.

No one but the old man who had seen the ring knew what Jack was planning on doing tonight. And many, Jack thought, wouldn't believe it. He'd told his friends so many times that he'd get married when he was fifty, so that someone could help take care of him as he got older. Sure, he dated, but rarely returned to the same place twice. Whenever he spoke of relationships, he compared them to skiing: Everyone thinks I should do it, that I'd be good at it, that it's so fun and enjoyable, but whenever I get up there, I just don't understand all the hype. I'm uncomfortable… my feet hurt… my face is numb, and all I want to do it get off the damn mountain. But here he was, facing his almost-fiancée, his almost wife-to-be. These were the last moments of his single days, and he wasn't sad about it. Never again would he have to pick up a girl at eight, make small talk over Italian food, or pretend to care for traveling or musicals. He'd never have to say "I'll call you" or "Had a great time" or "We have to talk" or "I think we just want different things" again.

A summer wind blew through the grassy area, causing napkins and plastic cups to escape their blankets. The boy got up and chased a wrapper through the crowd, and the father got up and chased the boy, and Jack chased the father and boy with his eyes.

Jack took a sip of champagne. "You know," he said. "I wasn't even going to talk to you that day at LAX."

"Really?"

"You aren't the kind of woman a guy can just talk to, you know, without an 'in' or something."

Polly laughed. Jack loved her laugh. Soft, but sincere enough to make him believe she thought he was funny.

"But then, after the 'Sports' page, and the fact that our seats were next to one another… I just felt it was, well, a gift, and you don't turn down a gift."

Polly rested her head against Jack's shoulder. "You're sweet," she said, opening her wallet and showing him the boarding pass from that day. She'd been saving it. Fifty years from now, he would ask to see it and it would still be there.

"I know why they call it United Airlines now." As soon as Jack said it, he desperately wished for a time machine, even a shoddy one where he might end up on front lines of the Confederacy.

Polly smiled, shaking her head.

"I know," Jack said. "Polly, I've been wanting to ask you something all night."

"Yes."

Jack's eyes stared straight into Polly's. He reached into his pocket, pulled out the black box and angled it towards her. Her mouth opened slightly and she set her champagne down. Jack could feel the gazes of many eyes burn into his back and face, but he didn't stray from Polly's big black pupils. When he went to open the box, he realized that he'd accidentally placed the hinges in the wrong direction, so the box would only open towards him; quickly, he spun the black box around and muttered, "They really should put arrows on these things." Polly smiled, placing her tongue, like she always did, between her teeth. It seemed like a professional portrait, Jack thought, where he could only see Polly. Everything else was blurred out of focus. "Polly West," he said, though he hadn't thought he'd go with her last name, "will you marry me?" Sax and the City played softly, complementing the moment with light chords and rhythm, nothing overpowering, just soft sounds that made Jack feel as though he was in a romantic comedy.

Polly's eyes brimmed with tears. "Yes!" she said. "Of course I'll marry you!" People clapped and cheered, and the saxophonist puffed out his cheeks and chest and held onto a note like he'd never be able to play it again. Polly and Jack kissed, and he slid the ring over her aubergine nail, down her smooth knuckle and secured it to the base of her finger. Part of the diamond glinted in the last moments of day. Once again people clapped, and the couple with the young boy and girl smiled at Jack and Polly, the father even offering a remark: "I get it," he said. "You'll see… the champagne, the picnics… it'll all slow down." The wife smiled. "It did for him, anyhow," she said, pointing to her husband. The old man and woman looked their way. "So happy for you," the old woman said. "It's nice for us to see that young love is still out there." "And I didn't say a word," the old man said, "I knew what you were planning, and I kept my mouth closed and tight." He smiled. "Congratulations."

Polly scooted closer to Jack on the plaid blanket. Some of her hair overflowed onto his shoulder. She held out her hand and splayed out her fingers. "Can't wait to tell my mom. She said you were a 'keeper' a long time ago."

The commotion eventually settled and a little while later, the baby girl awakened from her slumber. The father had tired eyes, but a nice face, a trusting face. The mother took the girl from the baby carrier. The baby blinked as her eyes adjusted to the surroundings.

"Doesn't she remind you of Sarah?" the old man asked his wife.

"Yes, a little," the old woman answered.

The teenagers only had one soda left, and Jack watched them both sip from the same can. The old couple split a cookie. The little boy tried to whistle. The action figure was soaked with fruit punch, making him look like he'd just slaughtered a lion in the Coliseum.

Polly reached into the picnic basket and pulled out her favorite sushi rolls. She passed the other container to Jack. "You really went all out," she said, mixing soy sauce into chunks of wasabi.

"One… two…" the mother said. "Put that down, sweetie," she told the boy. He'd grabbed a wallet from her purse and had tossed it high. Credit cards and change fell to the grass.

"Oh, dear," the old woman said. "*He* reminds me of Sarah."

Jack leaned in and gave Polly a sweet kiss on the cheek. He hadn't noticed, but she was wearing the same pearl earrings from that day at LAX. "You know," he said in a soft voice, "I used to see a scene like that and tremble—the idea of being married with kids. But now, with you, I can really—"

"I know what you mean," Polly said. "It still scares me."

"What?"

"They change everything… your body, your habits, your finances, your sleep, everything. I just feel like too often people have kids because it's the next step. The timing feels right—a person goes to college, meets a guy..."

"Sure, some do."

"Look at Alan and Jessica. Jessica never goes out anymore. And she seems more intense—bossy, even."

"I guess," Jack said, "but it's us."

"And if you talk to her, it's just swim lessons, rashes, Mommy and Me."

"That's Jessica, though."

"I would never want to become one of those mothers that can't do anything but talk about her kids."

"You'd always be you. You're not like other women."

Polly nodded.

Jack studied soy sauce saturating a few grains of rice in his container of sushi. He looked over at the family of four: The baby girl was sucking on her bottle, her eyes soft and not open more than a slit. The little boy was practicing tying his shoes two different ways: loop-swoop-pull and bunny-ears. He had more success with bunny-ears. The mother smiled at Jack. She wore little makeup, but was very pretty. The old woman took out a Thermos of coffee and poured two cups, and the teenage boy removed his sweater, gave it to his girlfriend, and tucked his arms into his t-shirt.

"I love you," Polly said.

"I love you, too."

After they finished their sushi, Polly pulled out two chocolate tarts.

"Can we split one?" Jack said. "I'm not too hungry."

"Sure."

They split a chocolate tart—one dessert, two forks—and listened to Sax and the City. Each musician seemed to have an extra hand, and when it came time for the saxophonist's solo, his fingers flew up and down the keys as though he was tickling his instrument. Jack looked above the band, at the sky, and watched the color shift from gray to black. The wind returned and pushed through the outdoor setting. Jack tightened his eyelids and savored the sounds of the sighing tall oaks. When another breeze came by, the little boy tossed up blades of grass that he'd been ripping up and storing in his little sweaty palms. The wind took some of them, but most ended up on his father's face and lap. The boy laughed, so did the father, and so did Jack.

Without even talking, the old couple seemed to know so much about one another—before the old woman sneezed, the old man was there with a handkerchief, and when the old man went to his back pocket to remove his pill case, the old woman was there, waiting with a bottle of uncapped water. All the necessities could be taken care of without uttering a single word; conversation was just a bonus. The old man draped a throw blanket over his wife's legs, one that was most likely made by their grandchildren, as it had names on it and was poorly stitched, and the old woman placed her head against her husband's shoulder. Her gray hair made sure there were no empty spaces.

Jack no longer thought of the future, but of the present. Polly's right, he thought... kids would change everything. It was funny as he had rarely thought of kids before, but now they loomed in his mind, seeming to occupy the blanket with him. He ran his hand over Polly's knee.

"I don't know if I've ever been this happy," Polly said. "I'm not sure even how to handle it. My mouth is going to be permanently stuck in a smile."

Jack nodded.

The teenage boy was reading his girlfriend's palm. "This one here," he said, "this long one means you're going to pass bio... and this here, this fat one, this means you're going to be cute until you're 82."

The girl laughed. "That's not even a line; it's a scar."

The mother rocked her baby girl, and the little boy lay down, resting his head on his father's leg, his eyes searching the night sky. With everyone pretty much finished eating, the conversations and noise died down. Just a smooth sax solo wavered through the California night. The father played with his boy's hair, brushing it away from his eyes, then towards his eyes, then against the grain, then with the grain. The boy laughed and Jack listened closely. The father took off his coat and folded it so that it could be used as a pillow, and propped it under the boy's head. "Thanks, Papa," the boy said. "It's warm."

Among the gentle notes of the sax and steady hum of distant crickets, Jack paid close attention to the father and son.

"Look at all the stars," the boy said.

"I know," the father said. "Do you see the Big Dipper? Right there." The father held out his finger and pointed to the sky.

"No," the boy said.

Jack looked up.

"It's a little hard to see because of the branches, but right there. Not far from the moon," the father said, turning the boy's head a touch.

"Oh," the boy said, "the thing that looks like a messy kite?"

"Yes," the father said, laughing. "And right next to it, right there, is the Little Dipper. They're really bright tonight."

Jack lay back on the blanket, felt the blades of grass contour to his body, savored the warm air that whispered over his face, and aligned his gaze with nothing but sky. One by one, he dragged his finger from star to star and connected the milky dots of the Big and Little Dippers, fixated on their messy, kite-like forms, amazed at how clearly they shone, certain he'd never seen them burn so brightly before.

DARK TIMBER

* * *

We were out hunting again. Deer, pheasant, rabbit, even squirrel. It was Dad, me, and my older brother, Roy. It was February, in the woods of the Sierra Nevadas, east of Sacramento, not too far from our house.

Every step, every move, was hard out there. We were in deep snow, off the trail, winding through trees with branches that ripped at our coats and knocked against the barrels of our rifles. The wind sliced through the timber, hit us straight in the face, blasted us so bad that I had to shut my eyes and keep my lids down tight. With the wind, though, came this nice smell, like the forest all in one swoop—fresh evergreen. I ran my hand over the bark of a pine. Even with my gloves on, I could feel the deep ridges. They were so tough, the trees. Tougher than anything. They'd been through it all—the below-zero winters, the frost and wind, the pitch-black nights. I wished they could have perfect weather for a few weeks. Take a good break.

"There's something," Roy said, pointing to the bushes. There was a lot of game on this side of the mountain. Dad had said the land was protected, but that the signs were covered up, so if we ran into anyone, just to play dumb. "There," Roy said again.

Dad inched closer to the bushes with both his rifle and shotgun slung over his back. It was a hard shot. A moving-target shot, Dad called it. You had to shoot in front of the animal and basically let it run into the bullet.

I wanted to yell out, help whatever was hiding.

Wind whipped through the woods, taking some falling snow with it. I was cold and scared. Roy didn't look like he was either of those things.

Dad bent down and picked up a small branch and threw it into the bushes. It rattled as it fell through. A large boar with bristly fur and tusks that looked like upside-down icicles darted across the powder, making sounds like it was snoring even though it was wide awake.

"Shoot," Dad said. "Shoot!"

I wanted to show Dad that I could pull the trigger, so I placed my rifle tight against my shoulder and put some pressure on the trigger, but as soon as I lined up with the boar's body, I knew I couldn't. Roy shot, but missed. The smell of gunpowder was strong and bitter and made my eyes water as I pulled in a deep breath. I tracked the boar. Watched its black body sprint over white ground. I bet it wished it wasn't black. I bet it wished it blended in better.

"Fire!" Dad shouted. "Dammit, Clevie. Shoot!"

I didn't. I couldn't.

Dad stomped over towards me, his boots crunching. I tensed up and tried making myself small by hunching my shoulders and bringing my head to my chest. Roy was looking at me, eyes big. Dad smacked me on the back of the head, hard, and I fell to the ground, slammed the corner of my lips against a rock hidden under the snow. Blood oozed from the cut, and I reached for it with my tongue. The taste was sweet. From the ground, I looked up at Dad, who was standing over me. He was huge. His mustache was black and frost had formed at the tips and he breathed out his nose in long, hard puffs. His eyes were blue like the sky, though—like the peaceful, clean sky.

"Goddamnit!" he said. "Why don't you shoot? Every time we come out here, you don't shoot! You don't want food?" Then he looked at Roy. "How many times do I have to say it, you don't shoot *at* an animal… you shoot *through* an animal."

Dad turned away and started down a hill. Roy helped me up, brushed some snow off my jacket and hat and said, "Don't worry. We'll get something."

I nodded.

I was a decent shot when I was shooting at targets or cans. Sometimes, I pretended the animals were sick, that I was helping them, that they were begging for me to kill them, to send them to heaven and let them run around with their friends and family. When I asked Roy if animals went to heaven, he said, "Yes. In every picture I ever seen of Jesus, He's surrounded by animals." But even with this whole thing in my imagination, I'd never been able to pull the trigger. Roy had killed some: a pheasant, a deer, and a couple possum. But he didn't like it neither. None of that mattered to Dad. He took us, said we didn't have a choice, that we had to learn to be real men so that one day we'd be able to take care of our families. I didn't want to be a man, though, if it meant being like Dad and killing things that never did nothing to me, that never would.

We stayed behind Dad. We were in deep forest. Dark timber, Dad called it—thick trees that stood tall and made it hard to see. Even though it was cold, the sun moved around in the sky and did its best to find cracks in the clouds so that it could beam its rays down to warm the treetops and snow-covered plants and bark.

Roy picked up a fallen leaf that had been packed in some snow. It was red and probably once flew high above on a branch. A deep vein ran right down the middle with smaller ones to the tips. Roy held it up to the sky and we noticed the way the light changed it from red to orange.

Dad pulled out his flask and took a few gulps. His Adam's apple moved up and down when he drank, like waves, and his nostrils got wide. He turned around and stared at us. His face was rectangular and his hair was real short. He had deep lines in his forehead that reminded me of a tic-tac-toe board and dimples big enough to hold dimes.

Mom had thought things would be different after Dad did his time at Sacramento County Jail—we all did. Sometimes it seemed like it worked, like when Dad sat in our room, his eyes big and blue, and talked to us about his dad, who'd died in Vietnam at the Battle of Hamburger Hill, something about friendly fire. But then there were nights like last night, when Roy poured out some of Dad's beer and whiskey. I was on my bunk reading *Call of the Wild* when I heard a bottle shatter and Dad shout, "Where is it? Where is it?" I snuck to the kitchen and stood a few feet behind Dad, staring at Mom and Roy. They pretended not to see me. Brown glass sparkled on the floor. A few of the pieces looked like states I'd learned about: Montana, Utah, and Nevada.

"Where's what?" Roy said, glaring right at Dad.

"Quit lying! Tell me where it is!" Dad said, leaving the doorframe, the space between them growing smaller and smaller. "Please, Dale," Mom said, touching Dad's big arm, but as soon as she did, he shook her off like some insect and she fell backwards and hit her shoulder against the fridge. The door on the fridge bounced open for a split second, and I saw a flash of light that reminded me of the burst of a rifle shot. "I hate you!" Roy said. "We were better off without you!" Dad took a few more hard steps. "Roy," I called out. Dad pulled his arm back, his fingers in a tight fist, then his hand cut through the air, and nailed Roy right on the cheek. I saw it in slow-motion: Roy's head snapped back, spit burst from his mouth, his legs wobbled, and he fell.

After a fight, the day seemed to die no matter the time. No one talked. The only thing left was to go to bed and hope for a dream. But that night, around two in the morning, I heard Dad in the bathroom. He was crying. It was hard to hear him good because of the wind, but when the gusts softened, I heard him.

Back on the hunt, behind me, Roy opened the chamber of his rifle. The noises guns made were cold and hard, like Dad's footsteps.

"Boys," Dad whispered. "It's something."

"What?" Roy asked. His cheek was fat and pressing his left eye closed.

Dad didn't answer.

Right there—not too far off, maybe fifteen yards—was a hare with brown fur and white spots that looked like freckles. Its back legs were all muscle and its tail was a big puff. I looked through the scope, watched it breathe and wiggle its black dot of a nose. All by itself on a mound of fresh snow, it was keeping still in a spot of winter sun, looking around with its wet marble eyes.

"Watch how I do it, boys. Nice and calm." Dad grabbed his shotgun from his back and brought the stock against his shoulder, closed his left eye, squinted his right one, and pulled the trigger—it all went so quick. He didn't waste time. Just aimed and fired and destroyed the hare, like an exploding balloon with red mist shooting in all directions. I felt sick.

"Come on," Dad said.

We made our way to the hare. It was on its side, packed with buckshot. Blood dripped from the body and stained the fur. Its glassy eyes were still open. I didn't say a word. Neither did Roy.

"When I was your age, I could've survived all by myself. No one needed to kill for me." Dad blew on his hands and skinned the hare, first working the blade around the legs, cutting the hide from its feet, then placing his hands under the skin and ripping the fur like an old t-shirt. The hare was purple, bloody, naked, and the way Dad dangled it, it looked like it was being hanged by its own soft fur.

Seeing the hare's eyes made me think of Mom and the night it happened. Dad hit Mom real hard and she lost one of her front teeth. The cops showed up. They knocked on the door with three solid strikes. Dad opened the door. "What do you want?" he said. He'd had a lot to drink. The cops were calm, though, and that seemed to make Dad angrier. He kept yelling. Roy was keeping me in our room. He'd rushed me in there and locked the door. A couple times, we pressed our heads to the carpet and tried to see as much as we could: six boots, four shiny black ones and Dad's two muddy ones with untied laces. We heard one of the cops tell Dad that he was under arrest, like he was happy to take Dad to jail. Mom was crying in bursts. I was too. Roy wasn't. He kept rubbing my back, making small circles on it, saying, "It'll be all right." One of the policemen took out his handcuffs; I remember the click—the jagged part sliding into the smooth part.

Roy told me one cold night when Dad was still away, made me swear on everything good that I'd never tell—that he was the one who'd called the cops. He told me he knew that Mom would never do nothing and that I was too young, said he had to do something.

After Dad was done skinning the hare, we headed back to the truck, where he wrapped the rabbit in a couple of black trash bags and plopped it on the front seat.

"We going home now?" I asked.

"No," said Dad. "Want to make sure I teach you boys how to hunt. It's been a long time since we've been out here together, the three of us men on the mountain."

As we started back up the hill, wind blew and trees seemed to wave their branches at us, surprised that people had made it this far to see them. I closed my eyes and listened to the gusts swoop through the trees. "Who?" the wind seemed to say. "Who?"

"Probably some better game on the other side," Dad said, "where it opens up on the valley."

The cold stung. My face tightened and my breath came out in big white clouds. Sometimes when my breath looked like that, I pretended I was a smoker. Roy did too. We'd hold our fingers to our lips and puff. Roy was a Marlboro man; I smoked Camels. We'd practice flicking our butts to the ground and stomping them out with our boots. Sometimes we did that, but not that day.

We walked over, close to the edge of a cliff, and looked around. "Take in that air," Dad said. "Feels good, right?" His chest got big, then flat, then big again. I took in the air and so did Roy. It burned the inside of my nostrils. The view was beautiful, though. Everything had been painted white: the sharp branches of trees, the rough surfaces of rocks, the pointy needles of pines. Everything as far as my eyes could see was smooth with snow. No tracks in the powder. No people on the mountain. This was what the Sierras must've looked like hundreds of years ago, I thought, with the Indians. On this mountain it could've been 1730 or 1850 or 1900—just the wind, the rustle of trees, and the songs of birds.

We stayed close together—Dad in front, Roy behind Dad, and then me behind Roy.

A few clouds scattered. A cone of light lit up a patch of trees in the distance. I wanted to bask in the warm shine, my arms spread out, the wind finding its way over my body and face. And then I saw myself on a boat, floating down the Russian River. Maybe a paddleboat, a sailboat, or even a motorboat. Then I was hiking with Mom and Roy. We stopped at the top of a hill and studied the sky, talked about the clouds, thought of things they looked like: "A cowboy hat," I said. "See it, guys? See it… the tall part and the wide brim?" Mom spotted another cloud, pointed to it, brought me and Roy tight against her body, close enough to smell her light soapy smell. "That one!" she said. "It looks like a bird! See the wings? There! See the beak?" Roy shook his head. "It doesn't look like a bird," he said. "It looks like a bat! See the ears?" We laughed, then we all laughed at Roy's laugh. I had a dog. One from the pound. Bobby. Bobby waited for me and Roy to step down off the big yellow bus. We went out to the apple fields, found an old branch and tossed it around. Dad came too. He was nice, asking questions about school and teasing Roy about girls. He pet Bobby nice and soft behind the ears, where he liked it, and ran his hand over his shiny black coat and watched the hairs part. He was relaxed. He drank soda. He watched TV with us.

In time, I left my daydream. I always liked daydreaming better than real dreaming—you couldn't control real dreaming. Sometimes I tried. When I was in bed, I'd try real hard to think of motorcycles or wolves or this girl named Robin who lived in the trailer park with us. But it never worked.

The three of us slowed down as we came to a creek that was almost frozen over. Parts hadn't made up their minds. Dad hopped over easily. Roy did the same, and then helped me across. Even though it was cold, I started to sweat. The climb up the hill was tough. My heart beat hard, like it might break my ribs, and my rifle was heavy in my hands.

"At the top," Dad said, "it'll open up on the valley. From there, we should have a decent shot at something." He grabbed his flask from his down vest and took a swig. A few drops slid down his face—they looked like dirty tears.

I wished that something would happen when we got to the valley, like another hunter would misfire and scare off all the animals, that I could still be with Mom in the kitchen, making brownies like when Dad was away, when Mom would put sugar in this little wire bowl and tap the side of it. I wished that we could sell all these guns, go out to dinner with the money, get fries and milkshakes. Tell stories at the table. I wished that no one I knew or liked would get hurt again. I wished so hard that I thought something would happen.

Roy zipped up his coat, bringing the zipper up a little at a time, so that Dad wouldn't yell about the noise. The trees were dark, especially the bark, which was almost black, and it was rough and scaly, like real dry skin.

Mom never talked bad about Dad. "Give it time, sweetheart. He's just not used to this life," she'd say, then she'd go on and say that he was a good man, that she'd known him forever and that she loved him. But she looked so tired now. Her lips were always cracking at the corners, and she had deep lines around her mouth and wrinkles that sat in the corners of her eyes. The scar on her cheek was easy to spot: the new skin was shiny and starting to look more and more like the letter *D*.

At the top of the hill, we stared into the valley. It was wide open, about two-hundred yards across, with only a few cedars in the middle—huddled together, trying to stay warm—and thick clusters of timber along each side. The snow that rested on the branches sparkled and, as the wind powered through, swirls of snow twirled across. Dad said this was a good place because the animals went from one side of the valley to the other in search of food.

We waited.

It felt good not to move.

I wondered about how many things had happened right here in this valley without anyone noticing. How many birds had learned to fly? How many shots had been fired? How many animals had taken their last breath on this snowy bank?

Dad removed his gloves for a second and placed his hand on my shoulder. I stared at his fingers. Hare blood had dried on his knuckles and was deep under his nails.

"Shhh," he said. Sticks snapped. Snow crunched. Something was coming. To me, it sounded like more than one thing.

And then it was there—a buck, a pretty big one. Its muscles thick under its brown pelt, and just nubs where its antlers used to sit. It looked like it knew everything about the woods.

Dad took his hand off my shoulder and we all watched the buck start across the valley. It had a long way to go to get to the other side. Dad usually wanted me or Roy to shoot, but this time he didn't turn around. He didn't tell either of us to get ready. He grabbed his rifle, shut his left eye, and took aim. Even though I wasn't shooting, I was nervous. I held my rifle tight against my chest, my palms sweaty on the barrel.

One second the valley was peaceful, snowy. Not a sound. The next, the crack of the gun, smoke rising from the barrel, the smell of gunpowder, the echo of the blast bouncing off the walls of the Sierras.

Dad got him. A shiver ran up my leg and a hot spike of vomit burned my throat, but I did my best to keep it down. The buck whined and staggered and made a choking sound. He dragged his body across the valley into the small cluster of trees that stood tall in the center. Along the way, he trampled bushes and scraped his hide against the cedars' bark. The buck then dropped to the ground and powder flew up as he struck the snow. Dad snapped the bolt of his rifle open and the spent cartridge fell between my boots. It was gold and smooth and sparkled in the sun; it reminded me of Mom's front tooth. The new one.

Roy didn't say anything. Neither did I. Dad brought his gun to his side and leaned on it like a stick. His face was purple. "I'm out of breath," he said. "Think I was holding it that whole time. You see, boys, I didn't panic. The buck was walking around, moving, but I took my time, focused. That's what you have to do. It's all about the gun. You get it lined up right, it'll do the rest. I just got us dinner for a long time."

We went down to see Dad's kill. The .308 had ripped open the buck's chest—a wound the size of Dad's hand. Scraps of skin lay on the snow. The buck's eyes were runny and the fur under its eyes was stained. I ran my hand over its coat, felt the thick hairs part; the skin was still warm. I couldn't breathe.

Dad took a gulp from his flask, then opened his small brown pack that was stuffed with another flask, binoculars, rounds, and his skinning tools. He scratched the side of his face hard, leaving three red lines that looked like whiskers. "Shit," he said, "forgot my knife and saw in the truck. You guys go get 'em. I'm beat."

As we headed up the hill, I looked back at Dad. He was standing next to the buck, leaning against a tree with a flask to his mouth. In between gulps, he breathed white puffs like a signal fire and ran his tongue over his teeth. He was proud, his chest out, his head high.

It didn't take long before we were at the truck, about twenty minutes, and back hiking the hill with the saw and skinning knife.

"Roy," I said, "I think things are gonna be better."

"Why?" he said.

"Just feel it. That's all. Dad just got a buck. I feel like it'll make him calmer, like he got the biggest thing, so now he can relax."

"Don't think so," Roy said. "Think this is the way things are… the way things are always gonna be."

We kept winding around cedars and Roy kicked a pine cone that was buried under some snow.

"He's getting better," I said.

"I miss the days when he was in jail," Roy said. "The place was quiet. Mom made tomato soup. Everything was better. I used to think that Mom would come get us, when he was locked up. She'd tell us to pack a bag and follow her. We'd pile in the Chevy and she'd put the truck in gear. We'd go and go. Head south to L.A. or Hollywood, someplace where the sun never stopped. And he'd be left behind, never to find us again."

"Come on, Roy. Don't say that."

"Aren't you tired of all this?"

As we got close to the top of the hill, we sat on the winding root of a cedar and caught our breath. Roy saw that he'd upset me, so he drew a couple wolves in the powder with the skinning knife. "That's us," he said. "Made you a little chubby. Sorry."

I smiled and pulled in a deep breath.

"What was that?" I said.

"Hurry," Roy said, getting to his feet.

We started the climb.

We heard it again. This time louder. They weren't noises we were used to, like hares or boar cutting their way through the forest. No, this was a growl that seemed to rip the valley apart.

"Come on!" Roy said.

I tried to stay behind him, but my legs were rubber and the wind was hard and the snow was soft.

"Hurry up!" Roy said, grabbing my arm and pulling me the last few feet.

We stood at the top of the hill. My hand shielded the wind that blew at my face and rushed past my ears. Roy pointed. "There!" he said.

Coming out of the dark timber on the right side of the valley, slinking across the snow was a mountain lion. I'd never seen one, except in books and on TV.

We were about eighty yards away, on top of the hill, staring down, as the mountain lion worked its thick paws through the snow and made its way towards Dad. It was huge, with most of its yellow coat covered in snow. Its shoulders were above its head; its jaw only inches from the ground.

Dad lined up his gun and pulled the trigger. Nothing. He was out of rounds. He patted his pockets. "Roy! Clevie!" he screamed.

Roy grabbed his rifle. I grabbed mine, too, and placed my right eye to the scope and put the mountain lion in my cross-hairs. My fingers twitched. You can do this, I said to myself. I watched the lion's large, wet nose move around and pick up the scent of the buck's blood. It opened its jaws, like it was trying to chew the smell, and I could swear I saw its big white teeth, jagged as the Sierras.

The lion had a strong walk, crouched low, and just when I was ready to pull the trigger, it changed its speed—went from creeping to running to charging, white powder flying in every direction. Dad screamed again, held his arms out and tried to make himself big, but the lion didn't stop, didn't slow down, kept charging, closing in on Dad, only about thirty yards away now.

Again, Dad screamed: "Roy! Clevie!"

It was a tough shot, a moving-target shot. I heard Dad's voice vibrate in my head: "Be a man, pull the trigger!" The lion was sprinting now, closing in, real close to Dad, but I locked on. Held it in my sight. Tracked it. I thought I had a good shot. I placed my gun ahead of the lion. Waited. Roy was waiting, too. Between the two of us, we could take it down. I squeezed. There was a loud blast and the rifle kicked at my shoulder. I stumbled back. Then Roy fired. He lost his balance, too, and fell right next to me.

Everything was quiet.

From the ground, I couldn't see much.

"Dad!" I shouted.

Me and Roy jumped up and rushed down the hill, stumbling through snow. The mountain lion was sprawled out, blood squirting onto the fresh snow, a few grunts and groans escaping his throat, but he was good as dead.

A few feet away, near the snowy trunk of a cedar, lay Dad, on his back, a ray of sun burning yellow on his red vest, his eyes searching the sky, a bullet deep in his neck, blood splattered on his face.

There was a quiet I'd never heard before. The birds afraid to chirp, the needles of pines and cedars still, and the animals hushed in the dark timber. Even the wind slowed down, softened its breath, and seemed to whisper as it whooshed past my ears.

I trembled and dropped my rifle to the snow. It landed without a sound. Next to me, Roy was pale, his eyes wide, his chest rising and sinking, white smoke coming from his mouth in spurts.

NEIGHBORS

* * *

Tiago Sandoval was a lifelong bachelor. Even though he was well-liked by both men and women, he considered human relationships to be a lot like exercise—a little a day. He was wealthy and owned a couple of restaurants in Santa Monica, both Cuban places: one with menus big as maps and twenty kinds of flan, and the other, an upscale place with starched tablecloths and flickering candles. He was fifty-seven, tall, with thin hair, a solid jaw, and white teeth. Women told him he had kind eyes.

For the last twenty years, he'd lived in the same house, a large two-story job on a seaside street. His house was the last one on the cul-de-sac and he had only one neighbor, Norma. Norma was about seventy-five now, though he'd thought of her as seventy-five for the last twenty years.

Last week, she'd told Tiago that she was leaving town to visit her son. She'd asked him to water her plants, collect her mail, dump chlorine in her hot tub (he never understood why she had one), and to keep an eye on things. Tiago had said no. He didn't want to be bogged down or responsible. A few years ago, when she'd asked him to do the same thing, he'd neglected to "feed" her orchids. She was fine with his decision, though, saying, "I'll have my granddaughter do it. She could probably use a change of scenery."

"I didn't know you had a granddaughter."

"Yes," Norma had said. "A wild one."

Tiago wished Norma well and headed back home. That afternoon, he sat in an ergonomic chair on his back porch. He stared at the ocean. The view was amazing now that he'd gone ahead and had a deck built. It was aligned with both stories of his home and spanned the entire length of the back façade. At the south end, he could stare down into Norma's yard—something he didn't want to do, so he kept a barbeque there—and at the north end, he had the world to himself.

* * *

A week later, Tiago had just returned from lunch service at La Havana, the cheaper of his two places. He stood in his driveway and sifted through his mail. The air was soft and warm, and he felt relaxed. His restaurants were doing well and he was home at two in the afternoon on a Tuesday. The other men of his neighborhood wore uncomfortable shoes, screamed on cell phones, studied the second hand, and waited to hop into foreign cars to rush home to overcooked food and stale conversation.

A truck the color of sawdust drove up the cul-de-sac. Tiago knew all the cars on the block. Lost, he thought. But the pickup didn't stop, didn't turn around. Instead, it swung into Norma's driveway. And then he remembered: the granddaughter.

The doors popped open. A young man and woman stepped out onto the driveway. Tiago stole a glace. The woman was pretty: shoulder-length sandy hair, big eyes, and pale skin. The man was strange-looking: patchy facial hair, a huge forehead, and a reddish complexion. Tiago went back to his mail.

"You're Tiago, right?" the woman said from Norma's driveway.

Tiago looked up, startled. "Yes."

"I'm Nash. My grandma always talks about you. Says you're a playboy."

Tiago laughed. "Your grandma tells me you're a bit of a wild thing."

Nash giggled. The man slammed down the tailgate.

Tiago and Nash walked off their driveways and met in the street. The man hung back, unloaded a couple bags, then plopped down on the tailgate.

"Nice to meet you," Nash said.

"Likewise," Tiago said.

"This is my boyfriend, Richie."

Richie gave Tiago a nod, and Tiago wondered when men stopped being men. What happened to the days when men looked people in the eye and wore clean shirts?

"Here to take care of your grandma's place?" Tiago said.

"Yeah," she said, popping some gum. "See ya 'round."

"Take care," Tiago said. He waved to the boyfriend who was too busy picking at his elbow to see him. Once inside, Tiago took off his shirt and assumed the position on the deck. He'd started reading *The Sun Also Rises* the day before and was eager to get back to it.

* * *

Later that night, after closing up La Havana, Tiago walked Maria, a waitress he'd casually been seeing, to her car. She wore tight jeans that squeezed her perfectly. He smiled, thinking how he'd seen her so many times without clothes. At her car, she unlocked the door, pulled it open and turned towards Tiago. "Bye, sweetie," she said. "I can come over tomorrow night if you want."

"All right," Tiago said.

She started her car, put it in gear, and drove off.

Things were getting nuts with Maria. He'd told her a couple months ago, before they first slept together: "I don't get serious. A lot of women like that about me. I'm nothing more than a good time—vacation sex without the hassle of buying a plane ticket." She'd smiled and seemed good with the whole thing, but he could tell she liked him more than he liked her.

It was almost midnight when Tiago pulled into his driveway. The street was dead. Only the coo of a confused bird. He went inside and checked his answering machine. Nothing important. After making himself a vodka tonic, he walked out onto his deck and stared at the sky. The longer he sat, the more the day seemed to evaporate.

He smelled the smoke of clove cigarettes drifting over from Norma's. He wasn't used to any action coming from her house, especially at this hour. The scent was warm, and Tiago drew it in. Then he heard crying. He got up, walked the deck, and stared over into Norma's yard. Nash had a towel wrapped around her and paced barefoot in the grass around the hot tub, a cell phone pressed to her ear. "I just wish you'd…" she said. "Please, Dad," she said. She then cried a little more.

After the phone call ended, she sank in a plastic chair and blotted her eyes with the towel, then reached for her clove cigarette that sat burning in a bowl on the ground. Her boyfriend came outside, wearing blue trunks, carrying a bottle of wine and two mugs. "Couldn't find glasses," he said, showing her the mugs. "What happened? Oh, God. Why do you still try with him?" He rubbed her shoulder, and in time, the two of them made it to the hot tub. The boyfriend got in quickly, while Nash took her time, making little sounds as the bubbling turquoise water came into contact with her cool skin. Once inside, she fanned her hair out over the wood and leaned her head against her boyfriend's shoulder.

Embarrassed for staring for so long, Tiago crawled along the deck back to his room. He closed the sliding door and told himself that he wouldn't do that again, unsure of why he'd done it in the first place.

He hopped in the shower and soaped up. Under the stream of hot water, his thoughts breathed and he didn't get in the way. At Nash's age, he'd had his first serious relationship with a girl named Eliza. Thirteen months later, Eliza had told Tiago she was pregnant and that she didn't want to keep the baby. Tiago and his parents and Eliza and her parents had sat down and talked it through. Eliza had cried. He could still see her shiny brown eyes. Everyone at the table had decided that Eliza was a woman and that she could make her own decisions. Tiago had agreed. In time, Eliza and Tiago broke up—too much seriousness for such a fragile thing.

He dried himself off and went to bed. The blades of the ceiling fan spun and he thought of things they looked like: spokes of a wheel, petals of a flower, limbs of a stick figure. Would he have had a boy or girl? What would he have named his child? What kind of dad would he have been? He turned in his sheets, unable to get comfortable.

* * *

The next morning, while Tiago was brewing some coffee, the doorbell chimed. It sounded so rarely that Tiago was confused. He tightened his robe, walked to the door, and pulled it open.

It was Nash. Her sandy hair was pinned atop her head with a pencil, and she wore glasses, a t-shirt, and pink pajama bottoms. She was barefoot, too. "Hi, Tiago," she said, like they'd been doing this for years. "Do you have any *real* coffee? All my grandma has is Sanka."

"Sure," he said, leading her to the kitchen.

"Oh, perfect, you're making some."

"Yeah," he said.

"I can just drink some with you... if you don't mind."

Just as Tiago was about to tell her "that he had a busy day and should be heading out," she went ahead and installed herself in the breakfast nook and began scanning the paper's headlines.

"Does your boyfriend want some?" Tiago asked.

"He's at work."

The coffee pot gurgled and steam curled to the ceiling. "Cream or sugar?"

"Both," Nash said, getting up and approaching the kitchen island where Tiago had laid out a quart of cream and some cubes of brown sugar. "You own restaurants, right?" she asked.

"Yeah. What do you do?"

"I lost my job recently. Now I'm back at school, night school. I know I'm old for it," Nash said.

"I'm old for a lot of things," Tiago said. "We'll be more comfortable on the deck."

Nash plopped on Tiago's ergonomic chair and folded her legs under her, yoga-style, and Tiago brought out a stool from the kitchen and sat beside her. He thought Nash had little regard for social norms, and that her approach with people was still very much a work in progress. She went through life, it seemed, with blithe freedom. Her age suggested she was a woman, but her turquoise-painted toes said otherwise.

"If I was you I'd sit out here all day," she said. "It's amazing." She pulled in a deep breath. "Life feels easier up here. Are there more smells or is it is just me? I'm getting eucalyptus and jasmine."

"It's mostly your grandma's garden."

"I know, right? She's obsessed with plants. Most of L.A.'s oxygen comes from her."

"What are you studying?" Tiago asked.

"Philosophy... I know... I know... what am I going to do with that?"

"Ha. You've heard it before."

"You have no idea."

"You're not there to get a job, though. You're there to get an education."

"Oh, can I steal that?"

"All yours."

Nash smiled and a dimple came to life on her left cheek.

"What philosophers do you like?" Tiago asked. "I studied some a long time ago, in high school... I can't remember much of it, so you could say anything and I'd be impressed."

She perched her coffee mug on her knee. "Socrates, Plato. So far we haven't studied that many. Oh, and Kant"—which she pronounced *can't*—"and Hume. I love Hume."

"I don't know Hume."

"Yeah, he's a cool guy, thinking of getting a quote of his tattooed on my foot."

"What's the quote?"

"He said, 'Reason is a slave to the passions.' Or something like that. Nice, right?"

Tiago nodded.

They sipped for a little while longer and didn't say much. A hummingbird came to the railing and fluttered its wings to hold still while it sucked out nectar from a summer lilac bush.

"Do you ever think hummingbirds get tired?" Nash asked, after the bird had flown off. "You know they probably get back to their nests and think, 'Man, can't someone build a ledge!'"

Tiago laughed and took another sip.

Nash got up, went to the kitchen, and returned with the coffee pot. She topped Tiago off, helped herself, and then sat back down.

Normally, after a certain amount of time had passed, Tiago's instinct was to deliver a closing line, something like, "Well, it's been nice having coffee with you" or "Better start getting ready for work" or "Big day on the horizon." But he didn't. He knew some of the servers and cooks would soon be arriving for lunch service at La Havana, but he figured they'd be all right.

"So you've never been married, right?" Nash asked.

"That's right," Tiago said.

"My grandma thinks it's weird. She talks about you at Thanksgiving and stuff. Our get-togethers aren't the most lively things, so sometimes I'll ask her how you are just to get her going."

"Oh, God."

"Don't worry, though. She really likes you. She always wraps it up with 'he's a good man... terrible he never found a woman.' I always said you were gay. But now I know you're not. I have great 'gaydar.' I'm excited that I'll have so much to share at the next family dinner."

"Anytime."

"How old are you?" she asked.

"Fifty-seven. The 'holy shit' age."

"What?"

"Whenever you tell someone you're fifty-seven and you've never been married, the first thing they say is *holy shit*!"

"Why didn't you? You probably had the chance a few times."

"Just wasn't for me. I've never been much of a relationship-type guy. If I got married, I'd want to be great at it, and I don't think I would be. There's this story about the Glenn Miller Band that I like. You probably don't know who they are, but they were a big-band group in the 40s. Anyhow, they had a show in some snowy place on Christmas Eve." Tiago took a sip. "They couldn't get a ride from the airport because the weather was so bad, so they had to walk a mile or so through the snow to get to the gig. They're carrying their instruments, wearing tuxes, freezing, and they pass in front of a house. There's a tree and ornaments and the whole family is opening gifts in front of the fireplace. It's perfect. A *Saturday Evening Post* thing." Nash clutched her coffee with both hands and put her feet on the wood. "The whole band is there, staring, and Glenn Miller looks at his guys and says, 'How do people live like that?'"

She smiled. "How many times have you told that story?"

"You have no idea."

"Did your family get along?"

"My dad passed when I was young. My mom raised me and my brother by herself."

"Sorry to ask so many questions. I do that sometimes. I just feel like if you don't get personal, you don't really have a friendship."

Tiago took a sip. His coffee had gone cold.

"Well," she said, "I gotta get going. Have a ten-page paper on Hume due tonight, and I've barely started."

"Sure, sure."

Nash brought the cups to the kitchen. "Thanks for the coffee. I can feel my body beginning to come to life."

Tiago opened the door and she walked the brick path. Dried leaves crunched under her bare feet like potato chips. A few seconds later, she turned around. "It's too bad," she said.

"What's that?" Tiago said.

"That you never got married, had kids. You'da been a cool dad."

"You don't know me."

"I can tell," she said. "Wish my dad was more like you." She waved and smiled, and Tiago held her in his gaze until she made it all the way home.

* * *

At La Havana, Tiago went behind the bar and poured himself a Pernod. *The Sun Also Rises* had made him in the mood for one. He drank and listened to the piped-in Celia Cruz. A few times he'd heard from people that he'd be a good father, but never from a young person. When he was a boy, whenever he met adults, saw their big faces and shook their big hands, he assumed they knew everything. When he was fifteen, he looked at twenty-year-olds like gods. Then, when he was twenty, he thought maybe thirty was the age when life became clear, but as his hair grayed and thinned, he began to understand there was never an age when life was easy—just an age where it became easier to pretend.

He drank more and thought of Eliza. She was living in Miami, married with children. He wondered if she ever thought about him and their baby.

Maria, the waitress, walked up to the bar. Her eyes blinked and her lips were wet. "Hi," she said. "Wanna get together tonight?"

"I'd love to," he said, "but I can't."

"Oh. Why?"

"I have company."

"You have company?"

"Yes."

"Who is it?" she asked, setting a tray of empty mojitos on counter. "Your brother?"

"No," Tiago said.

"Then who?"

"Family. A distant cousin."

"Oh."

"Yeah."

"Well, that's sweet. Soon though, okay?"

"Sure."

She walked back to the kitchen, the tray atop her shoulder.

Tiago went to the back of the restaurant, into his office, and closed the door. He sat at his desk, pulled out his cell, and dialed information. He asked for the number of Norma Lambert, his neighbor. The operator put him through. After a few rings, Nash picked up. Her voice was soft.

"Nash," he said. "Hey, it's Tiago."

"That's so weird… I was just thinking about you."

"Really?"

"Yeah. Just downloaded some Glenn Miller songs. Not bad for old stuff."

"You working on your paper?"

"Trying. You at work?"

"Yeah. Actually, I wanted to invite you and your boyfriend to my restaurant for dinner tonight. Maybe after you finish class."

"That'd be great." Her voice was high. "I finish up around eight."

"Perfect. My place is called Mariposa. It's—"

"The fancy one on Ocean."

"You know it?"

"Yeah, I've been by. Looks good."

"Well," Tiago said, "see you then."

"Hey, listen," she said. There was an explosion of sound: clarinets, trumpets, drums, bass. "Which song is it?"

"I didn't say *I* was Glenn Miller."

"It's 'The Nearness of You'... by far my favorite one." She hummed a few of the notes. "All right. See you later."

"Bye, Nash."

He hung up and opened his laptop. He listened to "The Nearness of You" a few times. After that, he called his manager at Mariposa and told him to prepare something special, that he had people coming to the restaurant. He spent more time in his office, reading about David Hume, whose theories were difficult to understand. Tiago read them out loud, thinking that uttering the words would actually help his comprehension. In particular, he liked the way Hume divided emotions into two categories: warm and cold.

***

Mariposa was always the restaurant Tiago wanted to have. It was one of those places that made a person seem better-looking just by being there. The bossa nova was soft, the cooking—or cuisine, rather—had received frame-able reviews, and the service was professional but never stuffy.

One table in the house rested in a little alcove surrounded by windows. Couples reserved it for their anniversaries; a few women had even blushed and said, "Yes" in the quaint space. At eight o'clock, Tiago had the table cleaned and topped with a sign that read "Reserved" in loopy lettering. One couple asked if they could sit there and Tiago apologized and turned down a sweaty bill-filled handshake.

Around eight thirty, Tiago thought he saw Nash and her boyfriend crossing the street. They were huddled together and her boyfriend was providing stylish support for her as she navigated the asphalt in high heels, but when they passed the window, Tiago couldn't believe he thought it was them. The woman wore a decadent black dress with a high slit. He imagined Nash would call it "bougie." He wondered what she'd wear. People always dressed up when they came to Mariposa, and he liked that. In fact, he had a jackets-for-men policy that many told him to get rid of because it wasn't inviting and current, but he insisted it stay in place, referencing the many men who entered La Havana in shorts and flip flops. Tiago still believed that under no circumstance other than the pool or beach was a man to show his feet.

He made the usual rounds, stopping by certain tables and spending a light moment with patrons. Drinks were refilled, questions were asked, jokes were shared.

Nash's table wore a crisp linen tablecloth that draped over the sides and flirted with the hardwood. The cutlery was shiny and straight and the family of forks to the left of the plates glinted in the warm candlelight.

Time passed.

Quarter to nine.

Nine.

Then nine fifteen.

Tiago walked over to his manager. "Any calls?" he asked.

"No, sir."

He nodded. "When it hits nine thirty, feel free to give the table away."

"Yes, sir."

Not long after, an older man and young woman came in. Normally Tiago would have walked them to their table, but instead he leaned against the bar and watched the manager lead the couple—whose names were probably something like Al and Tiffany—to their seats.

Nash was just being polite, Tiago thought. She didn't actually want to come. She'd talked it over with her boyfriend and they'd decided it wasn't for them. They were young. They didn't value French wines and slow-cooked meats.

There was such discomfort in caring for someone, and it'd been a long time since Tiago had felt this way. Nash was different. There was something fragile about her that told him that something bad would someday happen to her. He pictured her philosophy professor telling her to stay after class and holding her strongly against his desk, saw a bus totaling her car as she barreled through an intersection, then a picture of her getting lost on her way to Mariposa shook in his mind, and he imagined her driving around strange streets, her face hot and blood beating in her ears.

He needed to know if she was all right, if she was safe. He'd call and hang up when she answered. Out back, he pulled out his cell and redialed. The phone rang and rang until the machine clicked on. He called again. This time, he left a message: "Nash," he said, "it's Tiago, your neighbor. Listen, it's no big deal that you didn't come. Don't worry. I just want to make sure you're okay. Call me if you get this." He gave his cell number and carried on. "Oh, and I hope the paper went well. I'm sure it did. Hume's a cool guy. Talk to you later… and this afternoon it donned on me that I didn't give you any coffee, so feel free to come over tomorrow morning. Bye. Take care."

The rest of the service he waited for her call, even switched his cell from vibrate to the loudest ringer setting. But she never did.

When eleven o'clock came around and most of the guests were finishing up, Tiago left. He didn't say anything to the manager or barman. He just got in his car and rushed home. Traffic was fluid and he was back on his street within fifteen minutes. He parked alongside the curb and immediately inspected Nash's home. No lights whatsoever. No cars in the driveway. He no longer felt of his hunches as stupid, but as premonitions. He hurried to Nash's door and rang the bell. Once, twice, three times. He swung the golden knocker. He placed his face next to a partially opened window. "Nash," he called. "Hello? Anyone there?"

He headed back to his car, pulled into his garage, and shut the door behind him, just like he'd done so many times before. There were some eggs in the fridge, a book on the balcony, and a bottle of vodka on the counter. Everything would be fine.

Tiago let himself in and mixed a strong drink. Upstairs, he switched on the light and sipped his cocktail. The windows were open and he took deep breaths and savored the night sounds: the pulse of crickets, the hiss of sprinklers, the sigh of summer wind. There was another sound, though—intermittent and soft. He focused. He slid the deck door open and walked out. Some of the light from his bedroom spilled onto the porch, and over by the barbeque he saw a figure, sitting on the deck, knees up, head tucked down.

"Nash?" he said. Planks of wood moaned as he made his way over.

"I'm sorry," she said, her head still angled towards the ground. "I didn't know where to go. The gate was open. I just came up these stairs."

"It's fine."

Tiago sat down on the varnished wood, only a few inches from Nash. She smelled of peppermint. His eyes started adjusting to the darkness and her features came to life. Her sandy hair was voluminous, like it had been teased for minutes before being sprayed into place and her golden hoop earrings glimmered in what little light the moon offered. Her clothes, however, weren't dressy. She wore the same t-shirt and pajama bottoms from the morning.

"I went home... to my apartment," she said, "after class, to get some nice clothes. And... and Richie was there with a girl. This girl I used to work with. I should've known when he said he wanted to meet me at... I..."

Tiago scooted closer and put his arm around her.

Most of the crickets had stopped chirping. The sky was black with few stars and fewer clouds, and a plane climbed in the distance, its lights flashing. Nash picked her head up from her legs and looked over at Tiago. Her eyes were surrounded by blots of watery mascara.

"I wanted to call you, I just—"

Tiago couldn't find the words, just saying, "Shhh."

Nash wrapped her arms around his body and brought her head to his chest, while Tiago ran his hands over her shoulders and closed his eyes. "Shhh," he kept saying. "Shhh."

ZORBA'S

* * *

We drove through rain. Lisa put in one of her CDs. Ever since she learned she was pregnant, we listened to this classical stuff, music with instruments only found in period-piece movies—lutes and harps and mandolins. You couldn't sing along to it. I tried to "air mandolin." To no avail. But it did soothe. Lisa claimed the CDs were good for the baby. Research had been done. Our kid would emerge with a good ear. Something like that. Feeling already like a well-loved kid.

My hand rested on the shifter. We were stuck in traffic. Lisa's hand found its place atop mine. Her other hand rubbed her belly.

We were headed to Lisa's baby shower. One of those *nouveau* showers, where men were invited. Were men glad to be invited? Nobody asked.

"Nick," Lisa's voice cut through a lute, "do you have any new names?"

One month left and we still couldn't decide. We knew it was a boy. We weren't one of those "we want to be surprised" couples. I shook my head. "Sorry, sweetie. I've been reading that book you gave me. But, well..."

"I don't think you can call it reading if you do it sitting on the john."

Hormones. I hated them. "Still, I'm looking over the names."

"It's crazy that we still don't have a name. Are we unfit parents?"

"No… we're just taking our time. There's still plenty of it."

"That's what we said months ago. What about Joshua?" she asked.

"No!" I turned down the volume.

"Why? What do you have against Joshua?"

"I knew a Joshua in high school. He was an asshole."

"Don't swear in front of the baby, Nick."

I apologized. To her. To the baby.

"Nick, do you know a short cut or something? This traffic! We'll be late for our own shower!"

I shifted into third. We made our way down a side street. I was going 35, but it felt real fast. We took a speed bump too fast. I waited for the comment about hurting the baby. Research had been done.

"It's biblical, Nick. *Joshua.* How can you hate a name that's biblical?"

"I knew a guy, that's all. The Joshua I knew wasn't biblical."

"Just because the guy was an a-s-s." It was okay to spell curse words. But spelling took the punch out of them. I liked the words *bastard* and *son of a bitch*. They were too long to spell out.

"Would you name the baby Peter?" I asked.

"H-e-l-l no!"

"Exactly." I turned the music back up. Bach was getting frenetic.

"That's totally different, Nick. Peter's an ex. You can't name the baby after an ex."

"Why not? It's biblical—apostolic, even."

Lisa laughed. She grabbed my hand and placed it on her stomach. Her skin was tight and stretched. Her belly button had gone from an "innie" to an "outie." I clutched it. It felt like a raisin.

The pregnancy was real. The first three months (Lisa called it a trimester) were hard to believe because she wasn't showing. She said she was pregnant. People congratulated, but it didn't settle in. And then she packed on the pounds. A gut the size of Uncle Leroy's. The baby part still wasn't there, for me. Even though I'd read the books. Even after I attended breathing classes. Still no baby. Just Uncle Leroy.

We came to some orange cones. A man was out in the road holding a stop sign. He wore a slicker and galoshes. He thought he was important. Lisa thought so, too. "Roll down your window, Nick."

He popped his head in. His mustache was so thick it looked fake. All I could do was stare. It twisted as he spoke. "Congrats," he said to Lisa. "I noticed the tummy." His mustache needed to be wrung out. "Well," the man said, "I'm gonna be honest with y'all. This is a mess. A real mess. A few trees have fallen over and, well, it's gonna be a while. A long while. I reckon y'all back up and go another way. Again, congratulations beautiful." He winked at Lisa.

I put the window up. His 'stache nearly got caught. "What a strange man," I said. "Flirting right in front of me. What happened to men who only did that stuff in secret?"

"He was just being sweet," Lisa said. She pulled out her name book. The book was bookmarked with the most recent ultrasound.

"Men aren't sweet," I said.

Lisa changed CDs. Handel. If someone ever stole our car, they would think Lisa and I had quite the taste.

The rain pounded and quelled the music. Lisa made a discovery sound. "What do you think of Kelly?"

"Hate it."

"Really? Come on!"

"Yeah, I don't like hermaphroditic names—all those unisex ones. Alex, Drew, Tracy, Jamie. What about Frank? Do you like Frank?"

"Frank? Are you serious? Am I giving birth to a bridge player? Who did I marry? You just like Frank because of Sinatra."

We had a good laugh. Most of the roads were closed. Los Angeles just couldn't handle rain. People were baffled. The fauna bewildered.

The wipers struggled to keep up. The telephone lines spun like jump ropes. A branch lay, killed, in the middle of the road.

Lisa yelled: "Watch out!"

I pushed the brake pedal to the floor. The tires screamed. I put my hand in front of my wife and kid. Our Honda wiggled away. "I think we popped a tire," I said to Lisa.

"Oh, well," Lisa said. She was easy to be around when things weren't going well. "At least we're all safe," she said, rubbing her belly.

"Damn Los Angeles! The *trees* can't even handle the rain."

"There's a gas station," Lisa said.

I put on my hazard lights and wormed my way to the service station. I got out and walked the perimeter of the car. More than one was flat. Lisa rolled down the window. She knew. "Really bad?" she said.

"Not really bad. It's just the spare won't be enough."

"Are we going to miss the shower?"

"Why don't you call a friend to pick us up?"

"I didn't bring my phone. You know how afraid I am of cell-phone radiation for the baby."

"How 'bout a pay phone…"

"I don't know anyone's number by heart." Lisa turned off the Handel and delivered a few controlled puffs of air, just like the ones we learned about in Lamaze. "I can't even call the restaurant. I don't remember the name—something Italian. Marcello's? Mateo's? Mario's? Matucci's?"

"No more names. Please. Especially not Italian ones."

An attendant came over. "Shit, man," he said. I thought Lisa was going to tell him not to swear in front of the baby. "You hit somethin' pretty good." The man was wearing a poncho and water beads traced over the synthetic fabric.

"That can't be fixed, right?" I asked.

"Nah, bro. We can't patch that up. But those are pretty common tires. Let me go see if we have 'em in stock."

I got back into the car. I clicked the music back on. I knew I shouldn't be happy. But I was. Staring out the windshield, listening to Gregorian chants with my two favorite people. I didn't say this to Lisa. Every time I said romantic things, she just thought I was mocking her. That I didn't mean it. That I didn't care about the baby's name.

I pictured the baby shower: people holding baby clothes, blue balloons tied to the backs of chairs, men tapping their shoes, looking at their watches. I continued to stare out the window. Just me, Lisa, and my son, No Name.

The guy came back to the car. I cracked the window.

"Today's your lucky day," he said. He sucked back some loose snot.

"You think so?"

"Beauties. Bridgestone beauties. Wanna see 'em? Yeah, let me show 'em to you."

I didn't understand why he was so eager to show them to me, but I went along. We went to the back. He pointed them out. They were, well, tires. To make him happy I ran my hand alongside of them and felt the little, new-tire, rubber hairs.

"Well, man," he said, "there's a great Greek place over there. Just go have a meal, take your wife, and I'll come get you when we're done." The man smelled like a combination of cigarettes and sweat.

I thanked him. My task seemed simple enough. I pulled some old newspapers out of the trunk and held them over Lisa's head as we made our way to the Greek diner. "I've been craving Greek food," Lisa said. It was hard to get a gauge on her mood. Sure, she wanted to be at the shower. But part of her was relieved. She didn't have to feign excitement over bibs and "onesies."

Spending time with a pregnant Lisa reminded me of my days in college. She wasn't high, but she ate like a stoner. She craved like a stoner. She had the eccentric taste of a stoner.

On the diner's wall was a mural of Zorba the Greek—"Welcome to Zorba's" read a banner atop his curly hair.

"What do you think of Zorba for a name?" Lisa said, cracking a smile.

"I don't think it pairs well with Taylor. Big fan of the book, though. Can't really picture introducing him… 'Hi, I'm Nick. This is my wife, Lisa, and this is our son, Zorba… Zorba, shake the man's hand, please. Be a good little olive.'"

"Kids would call him 'Zebra.' You know how kids are. Always taking a name and doing stuff to it."

Lisa and I slid into a blue, vinyl booth. The walls were white and columns were scattered about the floor plan. They weren't real columns. The paint was chipping and brick poked through. A bust of Socrates stared at me. I wondered if he felt bad that he hadn't made it onto the outdoor mural. Was he pissed that he'd been beaten out by Zorba? He did look pensive. After all, it was he who said, "The unexamined life is not worth living."

A little kid came and delivered laminated menus. Mine had a piece of a hash brown stuck to it. The kid had smooth skin. He wore an adult-sized polo with all the buttons fastened, and his dark hair was parted down the middle and flopped over his ears. His smile was as large as his shirt. I wasn't great with ages, but I guessed he was probably eight or nine.

"You have such long eyelashes," Lisa said to the boy. "I'm jealous."

The kid looked at the floor. "Thank you. I'll be your waitress, I mean, waiter," he said, looking at his basketball sneakers. "Can I get you some drinks?"

"I'll take a coffee, sir."

"Water's fine," Lisa said.

The kid walked across the linoleum floor and tugged at his mom's apron. "One coffee, one water," he said.

A few years ago, Lisa would have started her "I want one" rant.

"He's so cute," she said. "Did you see his big eyes and little nails?" Lisa pulled out the baby-name book.

I didn't care about cute. I loved the honesty of children. The innocence. The way everything was new. The way the little ones' gums hadn't yet been pierced by teeth; the way they walked like my Uncle Leroy after a few whiskeys; the way they'd come right up to you and say "you smell" or "you're pretty."

"I wonder what his name is…" I said.

She was engrossed in her book. "You know I don't even know if I like the name Lisa. I mean, obviously, it's grown on me. But I don't like it… do you?"

This was a set-up. It sounded like a question, but it was a woman's ambush. "I love the name Lisa."

"That's sweet. I was hoping you'd say that. My parents almost named me Maggie. Can you believe that? Maggie?"

I didn't want to get into it. Maggie struck me as being a quality name, but Lisa wouldn't believe me.

The kid came back with our drinks. The liquids swayed like winter seas. I helped him with the coffee. He wasn't like other waiters. He didn't sport a salesman's smile or laugh at dumb jokes. After the drinks, he walked away and adjusted his underwear.

"Did you take their order?" his mom asked.

Lisa and I watched the kid and his mom talk; the mom licked her fingers and wiped a smudge from the boy's nose.

The rain pounded the diner and zigzagged down the windows. Drains filled with trash; water overflowed onto the sidewalk. Cars drove through the puddles and splashed Zorba's. The kid laughed every time it happened. I knew I was ready for fatherhood; his laugh did something to me.

"Hello," the kid said. "I can take your order."

"You're doing a great job," I said.

"Such a good boy," Lisa said. Whenever she spoke to children her voice went to another place. A high one. "I'll have the Odyssey Omelet with extra ham and Swiss cheese and no bell peppers."

He wrote something down. I wanted to get a look at his penmanship. He knew. He shielded it from me like a high school girl.

"For you?" he pointed at me. The pen looked massive in his hand.

"I'll have the Plato Pancakes with strawberries."

The kid tore off the ticket and walked away. His shoelaces were untied, and the plastic tips made little tapping noises. I watched him bring our order to his mom. He pulled the underwear out of his crack again.

I mixed in a little more cream. Lisa was scouring the book's pages; she'd even taken out a highlighter. It squeaked. "Ryan?"

"Too jocky…"

"You think?"

"Yeah, I can see the crew cut and the muscles. I can see the obligation to pick on nerds."

"I like it. It's new but not weird."

I didn't answer. Just took another sip and watched the dark sky. Lighting struck. The kid showed his mom where it had flashed. Thunder sounded. The boy's eyes widened. His mom whispered something to him and he laughed.

Lisa took a sip of water. "Hunter?" she asked.

"Maybe for a Golden Retriever."

"You're right. I'm losing it."

"Why don't we just each name the baby something?"

Lisa smiled.

"Sorry, Lisa… I just can't stand those names. You know the ones that stand for things, like Angel or Jesus or Bella or Joy or

Faith—the kid always grows up to become the polar opposite of the name."

"You're crazy, Nick."

"I'm serious. Angel becomes a gang member. Jesus becomes a maniacal atheist. Bella's ugly. Joy's manic-depressive. The only one of those names that delivers is Dick. People don't blame Dicks. They can't help it."

The food arrived. The mother carried the tray on her shoulder and the pot of coffee in her hand. She laid the food in front of us, while her son hid behind her frame. He poked his head out from time to time. "Enjoy your meal," the mother said.

Lisa waved at the boy and took a bite. He waved back. His cowlick pointed north. His mother licked her fingers again and smoothed it. In between bites, Lisa would deliver a name. I'd veto it. Then I would offer a name. She would shake her head. This went on for most of the meal.

A mirror with a Greek beer insignia hung in the middle of the restaurant. In its reflection I could see the kid reading a book. He was sitting on a blue chair. His feet dangled. The dirty laces hung to the floor. Lisa could see me looking over her freckled shoulder. She turned around and saw where my eyes were directed. She looked in the mirror, too, and stared at the quiet, reading boy. We took bites and sips. We didn't talk. Our eyes saw the same thing. Our minds played similar stories.

"Such an amazing boy," I said.

"He really is. I don't have to say 'I want one' anymore."

I drizzled syrup atop my cakes. Lisa couldn't stop eating. She never used to finish her meals, but these days, it was as though she was in a food competition. I remembered the Lisa from college, the one that called herself a *pescatarian*. I didn't know what that was. I thought it was a religious sect. These days any meat would do. She was a regular American glutton. You could see her on the news in the trans-fat stories.

When Lisa and I weren't talking about names, we discussed the living situation. Maybe it was time for a bigger place. Maybe it was time for a bigger income.

"How long has it been?" Lisa asked.

I looked at the clock on the wall. The hands were lightning bolts held by Zeus. It was hard to decipher the time. "It's been about half an hour, maybe forty minutes."

"Oh my God, Nick… we're an hour late for the shower!"

"It's fine. They're eating bruschetta. They're enjoying life. They know something's up. We're not the kind of people who do this kinda stuff."

"They're probably *really* worried. I bet my phone is ringing like mad. You really think there's bruschetta? Do you think there will be any when we get there?"

"You'll get all of the gifts and have to do none of the small talk."

"That's mean."

"The garage should be done soon," I said.

Lisa nodded.

"Harry?" I said.

"For *our* kid?"

"Yes."

"Nick, I know it's your father's name, and, don't get me wrong, I love your dad, but I can't do it. I really can't. It's borderline child abuse."

We finished up and pushed our plates to the center of the table. Lisa stacked the forks and put the paper napkins in the dishes. She always did that. The little boy poked his head out from the kitchen. He called his mom. They came to our table. The kid spoke up: "Did you like your Greek meal?" he asked. He tinkered with his underwear yet again.

"Great… thank you," Lisa said.

"What's your name?" I hoped this would solve all our problems. That Lisa would think me a genius. That people would ask us how we came up with this perfect name and we'd have this great story. Lisa leaned in. She had the same hope. I saw it on her face. Let this shit end—say something beautiful. Open your milk-mustached mouth, kid, and deliver us perfection.

He brought his eyes up. "My name is..."

"What was that?" Lisa asked. I had heard it. It wasn't pretty. Lisa had heard it too, but she needed to hear it again just to make sure.

The boy said it again. "Yehor."

We smiled.

Yehor set down the bill and walked back into the kitchen.

"S-h-i-t," Lisa said.

"S-h-i-t," I said.

"I thought that was going to be it," Lisa whispered. "I thought all of our troubles were over. That he was going to open those little red lips and that would be that. A single word. We'd have a great story." Her voice got louder. "This crazy day would finally make sense. They say God works in mysterious ways. I thought that this was going to be His way!"

"Trust me, I thought so too. Harry?"

"I'm not that desperate."

I tucked some money under the ketchup bottle and we got up. We waved good-bye to Yehor. We waved to his mother. The two of them waved as we walked out the door. We stood at the crosswalk and waited. The rain had relaxed. Inside, Yehor and his mother wiped down our table and reorganized the condiments. He looked up and waved. We did the same. Lisa really got into it. She looked like the whole Rose Parade.

The light changed and we began to walk. Rain's asshole brother, wind, showed up. I lowered my head and squinted. Lisa spoke up: "I just can't get over it, you know? I mean, he doesn't look like a Yehor."

"What exactly does a Yehor look like?"

"I don't know. I didn't even know that was a name." She tightened her coat. I put my arm around her, and we made our way across the street, over the puddles.

Our Honda was sitting in the lot, wearing its new Bridgestones. The attendant saw me and made his way over. "I was about to come and get you... good timing." His hands were covered in grease. I wondered if that kind of gunk could ever be removed.

"Excellent. Thank you so much, sir," I said. Lisa smiled at the man and got in the car. He smiled back. I followed the man into the garage and paid the bill. I looked at his uniform. A few of the buttons were missing and the collar was frayed. He pulled out the car keys and handed them to me. I looked at his tattered name patch. "Thank you, Hudson," I said.

"Those Bridgestones are gonna treat you nice. Take care." Hudson extended his hand. Oil and grime sat in the grooves of his palm. We shook.

I walked back to the car and looked at Lisa through the droplet-coated windshield. Her features were blurred, but I could see her tuck a few strands of hair behind her ear. She waved. A similar wave to the one she gave Yehor. It was cute and maternal. Only a yard away from the car, I waved back. I got in and turned the key. We drove off. The CD took a few seconds to load. As we pulled onto the street, a piccolo played. Lisa took my hand and placed it on her belly. I made small circles on it and slowed down as we came to a red light. I wanted the drive to last. The mood felt right. My mind felt clear. Things made sense. Life was slow and easy to process. I turned towards Lisa. With her free hand she worked the baby-name book.

"What do you think of Hudson?" I asked.

She repeated it a few times. "Hudson," she said. "Where did you get that?"

"Just kinda came to me."

"Hudson," she said. "Hudson Taylor." The corners of her mouth turned upward. Lisa tossed the book to the backseat. The light clicked green.

BLOWING OUT THE CANDLES

* * *

Walker slept the sleep of a teenage boy. Around noon, he awakened and stumbled to the bathroom. There, he found a note taped to the mirror: *Walker,* it said, *went with Bryan to the National Honor Society Conference. We will be home late. See you, Dad.*

Walker returned to his room, opened his closet and pulled out a pack of cigarettes that he kept stuffed in the tip of his right dress shoe. How often did a fifteen-year-old wear wingtips?

In the kitchen, he poured himself a glass of orange juice and then headed to the backyard. He lit a cigarette. Inhaled, exhaled. Life was easy today—no dad, no annoying older brother. He thought a little about what he would do after he graduated from high school. He wasn't really good at anything, and he wasn't really bad at anything. The idea of his own place sounded nice, though, a small apartment with a balcony where he could smoke when he pleased.

The phone rang. Walker continued to smoke, knowing the call wasn't for him. The machine clicked on: "Walker... please tell me you're there. Pick up!" Walker wasn't standing far from the machine, just on the other side of the window, so hearing his name warble through the glass, he gave his cigarette one last pull, tossed it over the fence and shuffled to the phone.

Bryan's "older brother, 4.0, Junior States of America" voice was annoying, so Walker picked up the phone. "Yeah," Walker said.

"Thanks for answering." Bryan sounded relieved. "I need you to do me a favor. I think I was nervous this morning because of all the big colleges and everything, so I forgot to go over to Mrs. Retton's."

"What do you need?"

"What do you have to get back to, Walker?"

"I was relaxing."

"*Relaxing*! You're always relaxing. Your life is one big Jacuzzi."

"I'm hanging up if you don't get to the point."

"Do you have a pen and paper?" Bryan's voice was sharp, like he'd drunk a bathtub of black coffee.

"Yes," Walker said, but he didn't.

"You know Mrs. Retton?" Bryan asked.

"Yeah, the old lady down the road—the one who looks like she's always sucking on something sour."

"I guess. She's been having tests done at a hospital for the past couple of days. She asked me to get her mail and turn on the heat, so she isn't cold upon her return."

"*Upon her return*... who are you?"

Bryan gave Walker some instructions and told him where the key was located. "And Walker... one more thing, don't do anything stupid, okay?"

"I'll be sure to piss all over the place."

"Come on!"

Walker hung up.

* * *

Walker didn't blame Mrs. Retton for asking Bryan to look after her home. He had one of those faces that looked like it belonged atop a Boy Scout's uniform, while Walker had one that seemed to best complement an orange jumpsuit.

She drove a Cadillac. That was the only thing that Walker really knew about her. He always heard the sound of the large engine and noticed the flash of her blinker as she turned up the street. An old burgundy DeVille with shiny wheels, mirror-like chrome and wax-swirled paint. A few times, Walker had waved to her, but she never waved back, never looked right or left, always kept her eyes straight ahead and pulled up her long driveway and into her garage that was located far behind her house. Walker wondered whether it was old age that made people miserable, or if some people were just miserable from the moment of conception.

Walker headed down the road with Mrs. Retton's key in his pocket. He remembered her husband, who was friendlier, always wearing a little tan hat and big dark glasses. He'd died about a year or so ago, around the same time that Walker's mom had passed from cancer. Dad had bought Mrs. Retton some flowers, and Walker remembered that Mrs. Retton had given them some flowers, too. Walker pictured the house during that time. All those flowers—it looked liked the botanical gardens. What a lousy consoling gift flowers were, Walker thought, an immediate reminder of how quickly something beautiful could fade.

Mrs. Retton's home was L-shaped and one story, as if the architect knew that an old woman would one day live there and didn't want her to have to climb stairs.

Walker jammed in the key.

The door opened to pink and soft-green couches, wooden furniture with golden trim, an old-fashioned wind-up Victrola, and a card table (whose green felt was topped with playing cards set up for a game of solitaire).

Walker's Nikes seemed out of place on the parquet floor. The furniture looked bored, having no one to support, no one to hold. The Oriental rug on which all of the furnishings rested looked museum-like, still wearing parallel vacuum streaks from the last cleaning. Pendulums swung on a multitude of clocks, and Walker wondered why a person who never had to be anywhere needed to be so aware of time.

He'd never seen a Victrola before, but he figured it out, and set the needle on the edge of a record marked *Strangers in the Night*. There were a few scratching and popping sounds at first, but in time, a voice came through. Walker had never heard of Frank Sinatra, but figured his mom would've known the lyrics since she loved old-man music.

As Walker explored, he encountered a thick scent of Bengay wherever he went. The smell was sweet, minty and medicinal. Black-and-white photos of a young Mr. and Mrs. Retton covered entire walls. Often, old people were described as "used to be pretty" or "you could tell that he or she used to be good-looking," but that wasn't the case with Mr. and Mrs. Retton. They'd both found the same ugliness. Both of them had noses too big for their faces and eyebrows that were too far apart.

The floorboards creaked as Walker continued to snoop, alerting the next patch of parquet that a new person was in the hallway. In what Walker thought to be Mrs. Retton's room, the carpeting was thick and difficult to walk on, and her bed looked like a relic from the Lincoln administration, stiff, with only a single pillow, and posts rising from all corners.

One of her dresser drawers was open and Walker peeked inside. There was an envelope stuffed with money. Walker peeled off a twenty-dollar bill and shoved it deep in his pocket, avoiding eye contact with a crucifix that hung on the wall. Then he slipped out of the bedroom and continued to snoop, but not before removing the needle from the record. The droning old man was starting to annoy him.

On the kitchen wall was the thermostat, and Walker, remembering that he was supposed to turn on the heat, moved the needle to the right and listened to the furnace bellow. He then opened the refrigerator. The bulb inside flickered and barely lit up the carton of milk and brown-spotted bananas.

Near the kitchen sink sat a telephone and an answering machine that flashed "2," and tacked on the wall next to the phone was a calendar from St. Joseph's Church, a Catholic church that wasn't more than a mile away. The top half of each month had a quote from the Bible, and each day on the bottom half had been crossed out with a marker.

Next to the kitchen was the den, and in the den was a wooden bar cart, complete with glasses and little sections in which to put maraschino cherries, olives, onions, and other weird stuff adults put in their drinks. Walker turned each bottle and read the labels: whiskey, vodka, gin, bourbon, vermouth, and rum. In a green Tanqueray bottle, he studied his reflection, which was stretched and blurry and made him already look drunk. He removed the bottle, sprawled on Mrs. Retton's plush daybed and took a few good swigs of the potent, warm liquid. His eyes floated about the room, and eventually settled on a painting above the fireplace in which Mr. and Mrs. Retton were all dressed up, their hands intertwined, their homely features showcased by oil on canvas.

Eventually, he closed his eyes and continued to drink and let the sounds of the quiet house find his ears.

* * *

"It's nice and warm in here."

Walker's eyelids opened and adjusted to the sun. The stuff in the green bottle was potent, and it took Walker a few seconds to remember where he was and what he was doing. He jumped from the daybed and placed the gin back in its proper spot on the bar cart as Mrs. Retton's footsteps neared.

Since she'd spoken, Walker gathered Mrs. Retton was with someone, but he only heard her steps. The blurry room continued to spin. Not knowing what to do, Walker wiggled under the daybed, encountering dust bunnies the size of real bunnies. Mrs. Retton headed into the kitchen, her keys jingling.

Walker did his best to stay still and soften his exhales. He heard the squeak of Mrs. Retton's permanent marker, and figured she was drawing X's on the days she'd been away.

Mrs. Retton sorted through the mail while Walker stayed tucked under the daybed and thought of how to escape. There were no doors in the den; he would have to pass the kitchen and there was a good chance that she would see him. What if she screamed and called the police or something?

"Bryan sent me, Mrs. Retton. He forgot that he had to go somewhere, and he wanted you to return to a warm home." Walker rehearsed the words, but too much time had passed.

Just then, Mrs. Retton came into the den and Walker recoiled and froze. She sat down on a recliner across from where he was hiding and continued to thumb through the mail. He parted the pleat in the daybed's skirt with his fingers. Mrs. Retton was dressed up. Old women were always dressed up, he thought, dressed up with no place to go. Her leather shoes reminded him of priest shoes—black and non-descript, and through the grayness of her hose, he examined her thick and ashy legs that were covered with old hairs that looked tired of having to grow.

In time, Mrs. Retton lumbered to the kitchen while Walker continued to lie in the dark, in the dust, planning his getaway. He poked his head out from under the daybed and scanned the area.

"You have two new messages," the robotic voice from Mrs. Retton's answering machine said, causing Walker to panic and recoil back where it was safe. The first one played: "Hi, Rose. This is Muriel from prayer group." Walker stuck his head out to get some air. "I wanted to wish you a happy birthday. We're both seventy-eight now. Can you believe it? Don't worry, I won't tell anyone if you won't." The lady giggled. "I hope you make that chocolate cake that you used to eat with your husband on your birthday. It sounded yummy. See you soon." The machine beeped. The second message began: "Mrs. Retton. This is Dr. Shields from Ridgecrest Memorial Hospital. I'm calling about the results of the tests you underwent this past weekend." There was a long pause, and the doctor hesitated to begin the next sentence. "It seems... well, I'd like you to come in to discuss your test results. Thank you." He left his number and told her to call right away. The machine beeped.

The clocks ticked, the refrigerator buzzed, and the furnace blew. Mrs. Retton shuffled to the den as though the simple task of walking had become too hard. Her breathing was strong, like she wasn't moving through the floor plan of her house, but climbing a steep hill. She plopped on the recliner, and it seemed to exhale with little bits of dust that floated up and sparkled with the sunlight that beamed through the shutters. Walker watched the particles disperse and eventually settle. Mrs. Retton tapped her shoes and held her old face in her old hands that wore rings and veins and spots.

She removed a pendant from her sweater and muttered something, and Walker remembered the poster on the wall of his history class, a picture of Martin Luther King with a quote underneath that he'd read many times: "Real character is seen in darkness, not light." Something like that. Looking at Mrs. Retton, with the sun coming through and touching and warming her, Walker couldn't help but wonder if she had good character, or if she was just well-acquainted with darkness.

She tugged a handkerchief from the sleeve of her sweater and dropped it onto the carpet, only a few feet from Walker's hiding place. Her hand patted different spots as she tried to rescue it. The hanky was monogrammed in black cursive. *Henry Retton,* Walker thought it read. Her arthritic fingers crept across the carpet in a desperate attempt to come into contact with the fabric, and eventually, she snatched it, removed her glasses, and dabbed her eyes.

The clocks chimed three times. Mrs. Retton sat for a while longer, only getting up to pour herself a drink. Vodka, Walker thought it was. Then she placed the glass back on the bar cart and scuffed down the hall.

He lay still until he couldn't hear a sound, then he squeezed out and tried to wake his feet that had gone numb. He moved a bit like Mrs. Retton, sliding and dragging his way to the front door. He passed the old pictures, passed a map of the United States with little pins in it, passed the potpourri that no longer smelled, and slipped out the door, locking it behind him with the spare key.

* * *

At home, Walker sat on a bench in his backyard and greedily puffed on a cigarette. With his smoke, he tried to make interesting designs, but everything just ended up looking like thin clouds. He pictured Mrs. Retton alone in her L-shaped house. He wondered what she was doing and for how long she had crossed out the days of the week. He stuffed his lighter and smokes back in his pocket and came into contact with something. He rubbed it to make sure it was there; he didn't want it to be. The twenty-dollar bill. He had stolen things before, but never had he stuck around to see the person, know the person.

Bryan's "student council" voice shook his brain. "Don't do anything stupid, okay?" Getting rid of the money would make him feel better, and being hungry, Walker thought about riding to the market to get a sandwich. The authorities actually had a name for spending stolen money. Money laundering, Walker thought it was called, or maybe he had misunderstood that episode of *CSI: Miami.*

He mounted Bryan's bike (his had a flat tire) and pedaled. The market was only a mile or so from his house, but time on the saddle allowed him to think. Walker heard the messages in his head: the one from Mrs. Retton's friend about the cake, and the following one, from her doctor. Walker saw her hand searching the ground for her husband's handkerchief, her veins plump and coming together like tributaries to a stream. He pedaled faster and harder. *I took the twenty before I knew her. And I only took twenty.* With each crank of the pedals, he distanced himself. The cold air buzzed his ears and tickled his face. He was going to buy a sandwich. He was going to forget about Mrs. Retton.

* * *

The automatic doors opened, and he walked inside the market and pulled a ticket at the deli. In his pocket, he wrestled with the bill, moving his sweaty fingers over its surface, hearing the soft crinkle and feeling the thickness of the money. *Today's Mrs. Retton's birthday. She's 78.*

The butcher called Walker's number.

"A meatloaf sandwich," Walker said.

"Everything on it?"

"Yes."

Walker watched the butcher slice open a roll. He couldn't wait to pay and get change that was covered with germs—anyone's germs but Mrs. Retton's.

"Here you are, pal," the butcher said. He called everyone "pal," even women. Walker pulled out the twenty. "Sorry, pal. My register's broken. You're gonna have to take it up front."

Walker grabbed his sandwich and headed across the shiny tile, under the fluorescent lights, and through the perfect pyramids of potatoes and avocados.

He passed by an old lady who weighed some apples on one of those big scales that was seldom used; her eyes were magnified due to her thick glasses, making her look permanently frightened. She reminded Walker of Mrs. Retton—all dressed up, her hair curly and white.

As Walker neared the checkout line, he noticed the bakery, first by smell, then by sight. Inside the bakery's display case were cakes, some tiered, others log-shaped, even a few molded to look like cars and superheroes. He stopped and spotted a nice, round, chocolate cake. He pictured Mrs. Retton sharing it with her husband.

"Hey," the baker said. "I've been calling you."

"Sorry," Walker said, "in my own world."

"Know what you mean. I've spent most of my life there." The baker smoothed out his mustache. "What can I get you?"

"How much is that cake?"

"Seventeen. And if you want something written on it, it's a couple bucks more."

Walker thought the cake would cheer Mrs. Retton up, add something light to her serious and solitary life. She might find it strange that Walker knew her birthday, but he would lie. That was something he was good at. In fact, Walker would just tell her that it was Bryan's idea, that he'd purchased it yesterday and had forgotten to bring it over. The credit wasn't the prize, killing his guilt was.

"Do you want it?" the baker asked.

"Sure."

"You want something written on it, too?"

"Seventeen bucks, right?"

"Yeah." The baker rolled up his sleeves. He had a tattoo of a whisk on his right forearm. "And a couple bucks more for a message."

Walker did the math. "Could you write happy birthday?"

The baker scratched his mutton chops. Walker thought it was strange that someone with so much hair was allowed to work around food for a living.

While the baker worked his piping bag, Walker, no longer having enough money to purchase his sandwich, strolled through a deserted aisle and stashed his hoagie behind some paper towels.

The baker curled the *y* on *Birthday* as Walker approached. Walker slid the twenty across the counter, and the baker held up the cake, wanting some acknowledgment for his artistic skill.

"Very nice," Walker said.

"I even drew a happy face... put a little too much icing in the bag."

The baker boxed the cake and rang Walker up.

The money was gone and Walker's guilt evaporated. *I spent it all on her. I ran an errand for her. In a way, I did her a favor.*

"Keep the change," Walker said to the baker as he turned. He didn't want the souvenir.

"Oh, I forgot to give you a balloon."

"What?"

"You get a free balloon with any purchase of a birthday cake. All I got are pink ones, though."

"No problem."

Walker returned to his bike, tied the balloon to his wrist, and set the cake in the bike's basket. He'd always made fun of Bryan's bike because of the wire basket, but today it made sense.

As he pedaled home, some teenagers drove past him and honked. He had it coming. A girly bike and pink balloon wasn't the best way to make friends.

He pedaled faster and harder and thought about Mrs. Retton. She'd be surprised. Since she was lonely, she might even ask him to join her. He pictured the two of them, sitting in the kitchen, talking, eating the evidence.

There was a slight downhill and Walker savored it, resting his legs, listening to the humming sound the tires made on the concrete. The chain on the bike bounced a little as he went over a speed bump and the balloon unraveled from his wrist. He slammed the pedal back and the bike stopped; he swiped, even grazed the string, but the helium was too strong, and the pink ball escaped, rocking back and forth as it floated up into the late-afternoon sky.

* * *

Walker returned home, a little sweaty, put Bryan's bike away, and changed his shirt. He opened the box and inspected the cake. A Mohawk of icing had formed in the center from the rough ride. Walker brought it to the kitchen and smoothed out the surface with a couple of knives. The *Birth* part of *Birthday* had been pushed together, so the cake now pretty much read *Happy Day*. Still good, Walker thought.

The smell of sugar rose to his nose as Walker made his way to Mrs. Retton's home. The scent brought Walker to a time when his mother was alive. He heard her sweet happy-birthday voice in his head, and remembered how she loved trick candles and allowed both Bryan and him to play hooky if their birthdays happened to fall on a school day. She wasn't around anymore, but their time together had been perfect until she got sick; Walker no longer felt sad about her death, knowing he'd rather have good memories than a shitty reality.

Careful not to trip or fall, Walker placed his feet soundly on Mrs. Retton's brick walkway. When he arrived at her welcome mat, he collected himself and brought his finger to the buzzer. He waited and watched bugs fly around her outdoor lights. He rang the buzzer again. "Mrs. Retton," he said. "Mrs. Retton, are you there? It's me, Walker... Bryan's brother."

Where could she be? He stepped off the front stoop and peered in one of the lighted windows, even tapped on it. "Mrs. Retton," he said, but the wind snatched his words.

He couldn't imagine she'd ignore a visitor, so he gathered something was wrong. Too much time with her mind, Walker guessed. He knew how dangerous the swirling of thoughts could be, how they moved quickly from storm to tornado.

Her extra house key was still in his pocket, and he removed it and slid it into the lock. When she saw him, she would be alarmed, but Walker didn't care. He had to know if she was all right. He hoped he would find her sleeping, trying to wash away the day's news with a good dream, a dream in which she and Mr. Retton relived a moment from one of the photos.

"Mrs. Retton," Walker said. His thin voice drifted through her home. "Mrs. Retton." The floors moaned as he crept into the kitchen and placed the cake in her refrigerator. "Mrs. Retton..."

On the kitchen counter was a bottle of vodka and a little glass that encased a single ice cube that was mostly melted. Next to the glass was a note atop a multitude of envelopes. Walker picked up the note and read the shaky blue cursive.

The envelopes underneath this note contain my final wishes. Walker read the front of the envelopes: *Will and Testament, St. Joseph's, Funeral Arrangements.* Walker continued to read. *After Henry died, I tried to sleep in the middle of the bed. I can't. I've tried and I don't want to any longer. This is the ending I want, Rose.*

Walker's fingers began to tremble and his breath sped up. He plucked the phone from the receiver and dialed, but he felt that time was being wasted. *What if she's still alive? Maybe I can save her.* He slammed the phone down and sprinted through the house, calling her name, popping his head in every room, wondering how she would have done it, how she was going to do it, and if he had done the right thing by leaving the phone to look for her.

Scared of what he would find behind each door, he braced himself for impact. But he found the rooms still and clean. "Mrs. Retton!"

Sweat sprouted from his pores and he could hear his heartbeat in his ears. "Mrs. Retton!" He approached her bedroom, and resisted for a second or two before pushing her door open. The light was off, and he strained to see any shape or form through the blackness, anything that would prepare him for the horror. His finger touched the switch on the wall and he flipped it. But the room was as he had found it earlier: bedspread crisp and tucked, the single pillow propped and perky.

Walker wiped his brow and thought about returning to the phone. He'd checked everywhere in the house; there was nothing else to be done. But there, through the back door, was the garage, the one place he hadn't looked. Maybe she had taken her car somewhere. He threw open the door and darted to the garage, crunching leaves and snapping twigs with each hurried step. A cool breeze blew over his face and dried new beads of perspiration. "Mrs. Retton!"

As he approached the garage, he heard the grumble of her idling Cadillac, even the sound of music.

He opened the door and was met with a thick cloud of fumes. Out of breath, Walker accidentally inhaled a good amount and began to cough and gag. He brought his sweater up to cover his mouth. "Mrs. Retton," he tried to scream.

Walker located the green button on the wall and pushed it. The garage door climbed, dusk entered, and exhaust dispersed. "Mrs. Retton!" His eyes stung and he rubbed them.

He pulled open the car door, and the cabin light came on, the bulb's glow soft and weak. The song that Walker had played on the Victrola earlier quavered from the car's speakers.

His throat burned and his lungs hurt. "Mrs. Retton! Please!" He reached over to shut off the engine and came into contact with her limp hand that was plopped over the gear shift. Her knobby fingers were cold and soft; Walker grabbed her hand and tried to find her pulse the way he'd learned in science class. He found her heartbeat was soft, infrequent, and exhausted.

Fresh air had now taken over the garage, and Mrs. Retton's chest began to tremble with each breath. Walker got in close to lift her, and as he did, her eyelids fluttered, her lips seemed to take shape, and her thumb began to make small circles on Walker's hand. "Henry," she said. "Henry."

Walker inspected her under the feeble shine of the cabin light, and noticed that pieces of soot had worked themselves into the deep wrinkles of her face. She wasn't wearing her glasses, and her short eyelashes had gathered black dust. Mrs. Retton wore diamond earrings and a gold necklace with one pearl that dangled perfectly in the hollow of her neck. "Henry," she mouthed.

Music filled the air: *Ever since that night, we've been together… Lovers at first sight, in love forever…*

Walker tried to lift her, but couldn't. He recognized the deep desire for relief, remembering his mother's final days—tubes in her mouth, needles lodged in her arms, her complexion as white as her gown. With care, Walker undid his hand from Mrs. Retton's, walked over to the garage-door button and studied its green glow before giving it a push.

Slowly—slat by slat—the door came down and snuffed out the day. Walker turned and closed the door behind him, hearing the muffled rumble of the engine. He stood outside and drew a deep breath.

WHEN MEN WORE HATS

* * *

Shin's hatchback rumbled as he waited for the traffic signal to click green. In the distance, the buildings of downtown Los Angeles shimmered like a galaxy, each glittering light, a bright star. He wondered if he'd ever be a part of this American solar system—if his star, too, could strongly gleam.

The light changed and Shin took off, though he didn't drive the usual route home. School had been tough today. When he'd decided to teach Chinese here in L.A., it had sounded easier. He remembered that Thursday at Donghua University, flipping through the glossy brochure with his English professor, studying the students' faces—big and happy with easy smiles—and he thought it would be fun. But now, five months into the school year, he just felt alone. His days were consumed with pronouncing simple Chinese words and hearing students giggle; his nights were focused on lesson planning and grading.

At the next light, he listened to his engine idle and picked up on the scent of stale coffee from his Thermos. His eyes wandered towards a small theater. The yellow marquee and big black letters looked tired. The sign read, AUDITIONS FOR A STREETCAR NAMED DESI E NOW TAKING PLACE. Shin found it funny that the "R" of "DESIRE" was missing, and he immediately thought of his Nainai, his grandmother. She'd passed when he was fourteen, but he remembered her well. She was an American lady from New Jersey with curly hair and dusty arms who'd fallen in love with Shin's grandfather and eventually moved to Pingyao. She and Shin were always close, and it was with her that he'd learned English. They always watched old movies, anything in black and white, and she'd told him that "love had gone to hell when men stopped wearing hats." Shin stared at the marquee for a few seconds before a honk ruined the moment. He hit the gas.

That night, while plugging a bunch of B's and C's into a spreadsheet on his computer, he opened the Internet and scrolled through photos of Marlon Brando. He stood up, walked across the room, and inspected himself in the mirror. "Marlon Brando," Shin said. The name did something to him. It was as though the man had been born to have that face, that career. He couldn't imagine Brando working at a school, filling out report cards, or wearing an orange vest while patrolling on lunch duty. He rushed to his bedroom and doffed his dress shirt and slacks for a white t-shirt and jeans. He wished he had a cigarette to complete the look, but he settled for a piece of chalk from his satchel.

His Nainai had always told him to stop thinking. Many times she'd said that he was too cautious, and that the best things in life always happened when you gave in to passion. So with that, he closed his laptop and headed out.

Once at the theater—the Fox Hole—he felt nervous and stupid for not having a plan. The entry was sticky, tugging at his shoes with each step. He approached the ticket booth, but it was empty. He yanked on the copper handle of the front door, which was shiny in only one spot, and pulled the door open.

Inside, it was as Shin imagined. For the first time, America matched up with his mind: high ceilings with ornate golden moldings, an overhanging balcony, and rows of empty red seats. He slinked into the back row and dropped onto a seat; puffs of dust escaped from the velvet and a mint crushed into powder under his right loafer.

Hot lights illuminated an empty stage and Shin's eyes canvassed the surroundings. Even bare, the stage's presence captured his attention—an ever-mesmerizing bright patch in a room of darkness, he thought.

"Elle!" A man's voice shouted from off-stage. He had a sing-song accent. "You ready?"

Shin sank. His back aligned with the seat's cushion.

The beat of Elle's high heels announced her arrival before her actual body, and in time, she was standing on stage, under white lights, clutching what looked to be a script. She wore tight jeans and a low-cut black tank-top. Her hair was reddish and grazed her oval face, and Shin thought she had to be Stella.

The man popped out from the right side of the stage. He was

short with a bald head that gave off a glaring reflection. His blue dress shirt seemed to be wet. "Where the hell's Ricky? What kind of guy does this?" the man said, putting his hands on his hips like a superhero and turning toward the audience. Shin hoped the stage lights would obscure the man's vision, but they didn't. "Ricky?" he said. "That you?"

Shin didn't answer.

Through the slit of the two seatbacks in front of him, Shin watched the man bring his hands up and place them around his eyes like a visor. "Who the hell is that? You! What the hell are you doing here?"

Shin stood. "Hi," he said. He knew his voice was soft. Earlier in the week, the principal of his school had told him that he always spoke like he was in a library.

"What're you doing here?" the man said again.

Shin's back grew hot, then his neck, and then his face. "I'm just here to watch."

The man let out a long breath. Elle brought her script down and ambled towards the edge of the stage. She whispered something to the man. Shin wiped his palms on his jeans and blotted his brow with the heel of his hand.

"Can you come up here and read?" Elle asked. Her voice was mellow.

"What?" Shin said.

"Well, our Stanley isn't here. He *never* comes on time, and I'd like to rehearse."

Shin didn't understand why the older man couldn't do it, but he agreed. As he walked the carpeted aisle, his nerves left their cages. He felt adrenaline wash through his veins and the burn of anxiety. He hoped his voice wouldn't wobble like it had on the first day of school.

Once on stage, Shin approached the man, whose brow was glossy and crisscrossed with expression lines that reminded him of the *hanzi* characters he tried to teach his students. The man shoved a script into Shin's belly, called out "page twelve," and gave him a solid pat on the back.

Elle turned Shin's way. She was a woman that always deserved a spotlight, Shin thought. She was older than he was, probably around thirty-five, he guessed, but her face still had the glow of a twenty-year-old. Crescent eyebrows hung over frosty eyes and a light smile played on her face. Shin thought she was lovely. That was his favorite American word. Lovely. His Nainai used it rarely, but when she did it meant she really liked someone. They introduced themselves and when Shin told Elle his name, she sang, "The shin bone's connected to the knee bone." He didn't understand it, but he laughed anyway.

Even though Shin expected his nerves to ruin the scene, they didn't. They gave him energy. He thought Elle was a perfect Stella, and he fed off her emotion. Shin felt American as he spouted Tennessee Williams's words. He yelled and paced and tried his best to remember the movie that he'd watched so many times. Sometimes, while delivering the lines, he felt he was Brando, the brooding gorilla, the twisted knot of passion. The louder he yelled, the harder Stella came back, and, at one point, when he leaned in to touch her, she ripped the collar of his t-shirt.

Towards the end of the scene, Elle wrapped her bare arms around him and ran her fingers through his hair. Shin remembered the line from the movie: "Don't ever leave me," he said. "Don't ever leave me, Baby."

The man approached, stepping over X's of blue tape and nodded in Shin's direction. "Have you done this before?" he asked.

"No," Shin said.

"Would you like to?"

"What about the other guy?"

"As an understudy."

A Chinese Brando, Shin thought. Like chow mein with ketchup. "Okay," he said.

They exchanged phone numbers, and the man told Shin to hang on to the script and memorize his lines. Shin nodded and hopped off the stage. When he was in the aisle and headed for the door, he glanced back at Elle. He thought he could see her smiling.

He left the theater thinking that Elle was fire—that on stage in her presence, he was at her hearth, hot and fixated on her glow, and that even outside, without her in sight, he could feel the distant flicker of her flames.

* * *

The next day, after school, Shin sat in his class, a cup of tepid coffee on his desk, a game of unwinnable solitaire on his computer. Class had gone better today. Shin thought that maybe he'd channeled some of his inner Brando.

He still had two hours before he had to be at rehearsal, but he couldn't wait. He dropped his students' quizzes in his desk drawer, lowered the shades, and rehearsed his lines. He pounded on his desk, then yelled, "Hey, toots! Canary bird, will you get out of the bathroom!" He got stronger each time he went through the script, and Shin thought there was something beautiful about Brando, even though he was nothing but a brute. He thought that every man could learn something from Stanley Kowalski. "You can't spell *passion* without *ass*," his Nainai used to say.

On the drive over to the Fox Hole, he didn't listen to music but instead went over his lines, trying to imagine the way Brando would drive and the way he would think. When a lady pulled out in front of him, he even called out, "Crazy broad," then thought about what he said and felt his face flush. He pulled into the lot and parked.

Soon after, there was a tap on his passenger-side window.

It was Elle. Shin didn't have power windows, so he leaned over and whipped the crank around.

"Hi," she said. "I'm so happy you decided to do this. Thought you might back out or something." In daylight, Shin thought she was even lovelier. It was as though her age was perfect for her, like there'd be no better year than the one she was in. He couldn't even imagine her at twenty-six. Everything had fallen into place at her age, with that haircut and that blouse. "The theater's not open yet. Do you mind if I have a seat?"

"Please," Shin said.

She opened the door and sat on a stack of memos, but Shin didn't say a word. Since being in America, he'd only gone on one date with a woman he'd met at the school district office. It hadn't gone badly, but it hadn't gone well either. She'd kept saying how quiet he was, and asking him if he was having a good time. He explained to her that he was still learning to be American and "fill in the white space." As much as he liked American women, they just seemed more accessible in photos and movies and on TV commercials.

Shin and Elle talked for a bit, lots of get-to-know-you stuff, which he liked. He also enjoyed being able to have a conversation while looking out the windshield; it was less intimidating than direct eye contact.

"You're a perfect Brando," Elle said, turning his way.

Shin tried to face her, but was restrained by his seatbelt.

Elle bit the corner of her lip and tried to swallow a laugh. "Do you want to run through some stuff before Gill gets here?"

"Who's Gill?"

"The director."

"Oh, okay. Yes."

They worked their way through different scenes. Shin found himself having trouble with the softer sections, the parts where he had to be less macho and more vulnerable, and Elle put her hand on his leg. He thought she smelled like a bakery, with just a hint of vanilla. She cleared her throat. "Can I ask you a question?"

"Sure," Shin said.

"Have you ever been in love?"

He was quiet.

She went on: "It's just because, for the quieter scenes, you might want to think of a time when you were *really* in love."

"I would know if I had, right?" he asked.

"Love's like Ellis Island… you never forget passing through," she said.

A few leaves fluttered from an old maple to the hood of Shin's car.

"That's funny," he said.

"What?"

"The maple leaf's a sign of good fortune in China. But here they're everywhere."

Elle grinned.

They ran through the scene a couple more times. Shin was

embarrassed for the way he'd answered her love question, feeling like he'd come off as such the anti-Brando.

Soon after, Gill, the director, pulled in. Once he got out of his car, he beckoned them with a quick wave of his hand and they all filed into the Fox Hole.

"Where's Ricky?" Elle asked.

Gill clicked on the lights. "I decided I want Shin to be my Stanley. I hate working with Ricky."

"Wonderful," she said, brushing hair away from her forehead.

Shin swallowed hard.

After they got situated, Gill showed Elle and Shin some of the sets he'd made with the help of his friend: a bedroom, a poker table, and a spiral staircase.

Rehearsal went smoothly, and Shin felt happy that he'd not only agreed to this, but that he was going to be the star of the show. He knew that his Nainai was behind it, and he thought that maybe he *should* act more and think less. She was always religious, and he wondered if she was out there, sitting in one of those plush red seats watching him, or if she was just hovering about the building. Why sit when you could fly? he thought.

Gill blocked out the scenes. His face was less sweaty today, but his t-shirt was still saturated. "I want you to come into the room and really own it," he said to Shin. "Like you're the baddest son of a bitch ever, like they could shoot you with a cannon ball and it would bounce off."

Shin listened. He swung the door open so hard it nearly ripped off the hinges. "Stella!" he screamed. His heart was percussive, and he relished the thumps.

Later, they moved on to the tender scenes. Shin softened his voice and wrapped his hands around Elle's face. Then, even though it wasn't in the script, he kissed her. She didn't pull away. She left her lips on his for seconds, and he savored the warmth. He closed his eyes, dug his hands into her lustrous hair, and drew in her ice-cream scent.

"Perfect!" Gill said. "If you feel it, go for it."

Just as Shin was about to apologize to Elle, she gripped his hand. And, still drunk on Brando, Shin squeezed back.

When rehearsal was over, they all walked out together, discussing who Gill had selected for other parts. "I just wanted to get my Stanley and Stella before casting the rest. It won't be hard. I know good people who've done this before." He locked the front door of the Fox Hole and they all headed to the lot.

A slender man was standing in front of Gill's car. It was difficult to see the man's features in the blackness. He smoked a cigarette and the red tip burned brightly against the night.

"Ricky?" Gill said. "What the hell are you doing here? I told you I didn't want you."

Gill quickly closed the space between them until the two men were only a foot apart. Elle hung back.

"Fuck you," Ricky said. His voice was slurred.

Shin left the warmth of Elle's side and wedged himself between the two men. Ricky's chest was stiff.

"*This* is the guy?" Ricky pointed at Shin. "*This* is the fucker that's replaced me?"

Gill didn't look scared. Even though he was smaller and older, he held his ground and stared at Ricky. "You're terrific, Ricky, but I don't want a headache."

Ricky turned around and Shin softened his hold of both men, bringing his arms to his sides. He glanced at Elle. She stood by her car. "Shin!" she shouted.

Ricky threw a punch that landed directly on Shin's forehead. Even though his English was perfect, Shin swore in Chinese. He dropped to the concrete and shielded his face with his hands.

"Come on, ninja," Ricky said, giving him space to get up.

Gill shouted for Ricky to "calm down" and "let it go," but none of it worked.

Shin wanted badly for this to play out like a Hollywood movie, with rain coming down, Elle gasping, and Ricky's body ending up in a pile between two parking spaces.

He ran a finger over his brow and felt a thin rill of blood. He pressed forward, pushed himself off the ground, felt bits of asphalt dig into his fleshy palms, and tried to stand. Once again, he collapsed. He heard Ricky laugh and Gill yell "stupid bastard." He didn't hear anything from Elle.

Everything slowed down. The rush of traffic was still there, though, consistent and fluid, and Shin thought it sounded like the surf of the Pacific.

* * *

Shin woke up in his bed with all the lights of his bedroom glowing yellow. On the nightstand was a bag of frozen corn, a bucket of ice, and a couple dishtowels. There was a sharp ache in his forehead.

"Shin," a voice said.

Elle got up and her face hovered over him like a mobile. She told him what had happened, that he'd passed out from the hit and that she'd taken him to the hospital. She and Gill had taken care of his car; it was all going to be okay. "The doctor told me not to let anything happen to you," she said. "I popped open your wallet, found your address, and took you home. I grabbed your keys from your jacket. Pretty proud of myself." She sat on the edge of his bed.

Shin ran his bare leg against the sheet and surmised that she'd removed his jeans. He hoped he wasn't wearing silly boxers. Why did Americans have such funny underwear?

"Are you feeling better?" She scooted closer and pressed a dishtowel filled with ice against his temple.

"Yes," he said.

Shin thought that Elle didn't fit his room. The cheap furniture and bare walls didn't seem to complement a woman like her, and then he thought that the only difference between the Shins of the world and the Brandos of it was that the Brandos weren't afraid to say what the Shins thought. And then, maybe due to his head, he told her this and she turned rosy. Soon after, she kissed him.

He kissed her back and Elle kicked off her heels. On his twin bed, they made room for one another. His lips started on hers, then migrated to the side of her neck. Her pulse throbbed. She moved fast, peeling off his clothes and then hers. When she finally undid her crimson bra and tossed it to the floor, Shin took notice of the triangular tan lines that outlined her breasts. Not even the sun has made it here, he thought. It'd been a long time since Shin had made love, and he thought that maybe he'd forgotten how to do it, but Elle's stuttered breaths and pointed toes quickly quelled his anxiety.

Afterwards, they lay in a mess of wrinkled sheets.

"I'm such a blend of pain and happiness right now," Shin said.

"Yin and yang," Elle said.

She turned the other way and Shin rolled with her, placing his hands in the no-man's land of warm skin between her belly button and soft tufts of pubic hair. He closed his eyes. He felt her stomach quiver.

* * *

As the weeks passed, Shin became a more confident teacher. Sure, he was less prepared, but his natural zest for life and his made-up story about his injury and how he'd "protected an old man from a mugger" made him an instant favorite at Washington High.

That day during lunch, Shin searched Elle's acting credits online. She'd performed some of Nainai's favorites: *All My Sons, Guys and Dolls*, and *Bye Bye Birdie*. He even found her real age, thirty-eight, on one invasive site.

The play was going perfectly. They were only a week away from opening night and Gill often told Shin that he "showed promise as an actor, and that he could feel real chemistry between Stella and Stanley."

Elle and Shin made love almost twice a week, usually when Gill cut rehearsal short. Last night, after they'd finished, Elle told Shin that he was the best listener she'd ever known. "That he did it with his entire body." Then she talked a little about love, saying that most people wanted a "Norman Rockwell life," and that she just wanted a "*Normal* Rockwell one." Shin didn't know what she was talking about, but he agreed with her.

* * *

On opening night, a Friday, Shin was so excited he called in sick. Since he'd started at the school, he hadn't missed a day. He called Elle, too, but she didn't pick up, and he didn't leave a message. Still, minutes later, she sent him a text about how nervous she was.

That day, he paced around all eight-hundred square feet of his studio, rehearsing scenes, visualizing himself on stage. He envisioned the audience staring his way, fascinated with his every move. Nainai would be proud. If she were alive, he thought, she'd already be in line.

Each hour, Shin went into countdown mode and, at quarter to three, he decided to head to the theater. He'd feel better at the Fox Hole.

Since it was early, Shin drove slowly. There were winds—Santa Anas, he'd heard someone call them—that were brash and angry, but at the same time, sweet and warm. He thought that they were a harmonious blend of Stella and Stanley.

He arrived at the theater, parked, and headed inside. Gill read a newspaper in the last row of seats. His face was unshaven and pale. "Opening night," Gill said. "I get like this."

Backstage, Shin ran his hand over the thick folds of the burgundy curtain and brushed the heavy material. Then he went into the ladies' dressing room. He picked up one of Elle's dresses and smelled the fabric. Her dress was laced with the same sugary scent as his sheets, and he pulled in another whiff. He couldn't stop thinking about her; it made him feel better that she was in the world—that when he was a boy in Pingyao, she was already a lady in L.A. She was perfect and funny, and he loved that more than anything she didn't think she was perfect or funny. He would constantly have to give her pep talks, which only seemed to make her like him more. He spent time on them, actually, thinking that if he could say the right thing, hit the right note like Tennessee Williams or Brando, she could love him, too. He needed that gaze to be his forever—the way she looked at him on stage, when the lights were hot and the theater was still.

* * *

Minutes before showtime, the cast met backstage and each member said a variant of "good luck." Shin preferred the days when it was just him and Elle, but now the cast was all filled in, and the set was noisier and crowded. He did catch up with Elle, placed his hand on the small of her back, and wished her luck. "I love you," he said.

She kissed him. "I'll always love you," she said.

* * *

Those words helped transform Shin from Chinese teacher to a devil-may-care heartthrob. On stage, he oozed machismo. The lines came to him like he'd written them, and he felt he spouted them even better than Brando. His hot face dripped sweat like a beast. The scene drew applause from the smallish crowd during a break in dialogue. A few times, Shin even called Stella "Stell." As he charged off-stage, he thought L.A. really was a town full of maple leaves.

"Brilliant," Gill said. "I love the way you threw the glass. You're Brando now!"

Shin listened to a scene between Blanche and Stella. He wondered if Hollywood people fell in love to make movies better. The scenes were deeper, and he couldn't wait to take the stage again just to see Elle's face.

In Act Two, Shin put together another solid performance. He felt so confident in his movements that he thought the crowd would buy him doing just about anything. He took his time with his lines, savoring the thick moments of quiet. He heard a woman gasp and another shout, "Oh, dear," the way Nainai used to.

The play came to a close, and Shin watched Elle weep. He remembered reading in the script that Stella was to cry "luxurious tears." And she did just that, produced viscous droplets that traced her cheeks. Shin wanted to scoop them up with his tongue, whisper to her that everything would be fine, but he stayed true to Stanley Kowalski. That was one thing he liked better about the play than the movie—in the movie, Stella left Stanley; in the play, Stella stayed.

The crowd offered a loud ovation. What they lacked in size they made up for in enthusiasm. Shin and Elle were introduced last, and they held hands and bowed simultaneously. Then Gill popped out from stage-left and waved.

Slowly, the curtain dragged its body along the hardwood and closed. Shin and Elle stood behind it for a few seconds before embracing. The crowd filed out. "My Stanley," Elle said, running her bony fingers around Shin's jaw.

"Do you want to come over?" Shin asked.

"Of course," Elle said. "Come by my dressing room after you get changed."

Shin ran a hand through his hair and smiled.

They turned and walked to their dressing rooms. Shin didn't want to just take her back to his place; he wanted to do something a little more celebratory, like grab a drink at a fancy beachside bar, one of those places that called outside "alfresco." Elle always talked about this drink called Chartreuse, and he finally wanted to taste it.

He changed in his dressing room. His pulse returned to normal, and his skin did away with its reddish hue. A few members of the cast—Blanche, Pablo, and Steve—came by and offered their congratulations. They laughed and said they preferred working with him over Ricky.

The theater transformed from Times Square to Nebraska in a matter of minutes. Finally, Shin walked over to her dressing room. The door was closed. He knocked hard. "Stell!" he called out, then laughed.

The door was pulled open by a solid man in a dark blue suit. He had hazel eyes and closely cropped hair. A little girl with feathery bangs stood alongside him. Elle sat on a stool towards the back of the room, facing her makeup mirror, which was framed by a multitude of hot, naked light bulbs.

"I'm Todd," the man said. "You were terrific. A passionate S.O.B."

"Thanks," Shin said.

The two men shook hands.

Elle spun herself around and faced Shin, though she didn't

bring her eyes up to meet his. Instead, her gaze lined up with the tips of Shin's dress shoes. Her cheeks were shiny. "They surprised me," she said softly.

Todd ran his tongue over his large lips. "She can't believe it. Lela and I were supposed to visit my mom up north, but we couldn't miss this… so we made a U-turn by Fresno."

Todd kept talking, his low voice droning. Even though Shin had gathered all the necessary information, he still believed that at any moment Todd and the little girl would clear out and shut the door behind them, leaving Stanley and Stella to celebrate. He took in the rose petals that were scattered about the room, collateral damage from casually handling bouquet after bouquet. Then Shin stared at Elle's crossed legs. Only days before were those long limbs coiled in his blue sheets.

"Well," Shin finally said when Todd took a breath, "I'm off."

Elle threw him one last smile, and he savored the curl of her thin lips and the flash of her delicate teeth.

"My mommy's an actress," the little girl said.

"A really good one," Shin added.

He turned and headed for the exit, hoping Elle would dash after him as she had on this stage only thirty minutes prior. He slowed his gait to give her time, but a sound never escaped the walls of her dressing room. A ripping sensation came over Shin, though, a clawing inside his chest and stomach that made it hard for him to breathe. But he pressed on, thought of Brando, felt the man's strong grip, cocky stare, and allowed Stanley's fight to wash over him. He continued downstage, slipped through the curtain, and left the Fox Hole.

CHASING LIGHT

* * *

I know it's not polite to talk about oneself, but it may do me good to share: My name is Conrad Ingalls. I'm sixty-six, a retired photographer, and married to the love of my life, Karen. We've been together for thirty-nine years, have no children, and live off the coast of Los Angeles, on the island of Santa Catalina. You may know the song: "Twenty-six miles across the sea, Santa Catalina is a-waitin' for me…"

We both wanted to slow things down after a long stint in the city, so we moved out here where we used to vacation and bought a good-sized place on stilts over the lapping water. Karen works as a first-grade aide at the only elementary school in town, and I pass the time like I'm doing right now—out on my small boat, tracing the perimeter of the island. It's early January and when I turn the skiff too sharply, the cold spray finds my face, and I let the beads ski down my skin.

My whole professional life has been spent with a camera around my neck, always trying to capture beauty and elicit emotion with a quick snap of my shutter. I've worked for fashion magazines and car journals, but mostly nature-themed publications. Recently, a few people who work for Catalina's tourism office asked me to photograph some of the island's nature to showcase on their website. They want pictures of gray whales, dolphins, California quail, and the elusive Catalina fox.

This quiet used to bring peace. Now it brings thoughts. I don't love Karen like before. I sometimes stare at her as she leaves for work and think about touching and kissing her, but I can't.

On a cluster of rocks ahead, I spot a flock of Spotted Towhees. Even though the weather is chilly and the sky is dark and looks to be brewing a storm, the sea is calm. The outboard motor hums at a high-pitch until I release my hand from the throttle and use the momentum to coast. When the ocean ebbs, chirps from the birds pepper the air, and I position my camera and wait for the boat to steady. The Towhees' reddish bellies are in sharp contrast with the pale rocks. I twist my lens and focus on the flock, blur out the surroundings, and pop off a couple shots.

I'm at the western tip of the island, where only an old mansion sits. Rumor has it, it used to belong to some wealthy man who brought his mistresses out here every so often, a Mr. Montgomery. These days, it's just a rental property reserved for spendthrifts who can drop a few grand per week.

The gigantic windows that face the water are usually covered with thick shades, but today the blinds are up. A hundred yards out or so, I bring my binoculars to my eyes, drag the two circles over the home, and inspect the façade. Underneath the windows are flower boxes stuffed with pink petunias and white impatiens.

I inspect the porch and am startled when a bright light cuts on against the steely sky. In time, a man slips into focus and leans against the glass. He's perfectly centered, like he's the subject of a portrait. He seems handsome, too, with an ashen complexion and a cigarette in his mouth. I keep my binoculars steady. When he exhales, large gray puffs, like smoke signals, float up, and I wonder what the message reads. He blots his eyes with a tissue. Is he crying? I wonder. It comforts me to think that sadness can find any of us. Even the handsome. Even the young.

* * *

After a thirty-minute ride to the southern point of the island, I'm home. I dock my boat and go inside. The house is warm and Karen is making spaghetti. The television is on in the living room and some shiny reporter is feigning compassion. I say hi to Karen and she turns and smiles and asks how my day was. I tell her it was fine. She removes a noodle from the boiling water with a fork, blows on it, coils it into her mouth, and lets me know that supper will be ready soon.

Dinner used to be just dinner, but these days, it's the longest that Karen and I sit together, and it makes me nervous, like I'm a tourist in my own town.

I go upstairs, wash my hands, and change into my pajamas.

Then I take a look at my shots from the day: a few flukes and dorsal fins of dolphins, a Horned Lark, those Spotted Towhees, and no fox.

In little time, we're eating in front of the TV. This started recently and I don't mind. The humdrum reporting fills the air and Karen and I eat, nod, and occasionally comment.

"Did I overcook the spaghetti?" she asks.

"No," I say. "You look a little tired."

"Yeah. I think I need a new mattress. It hits me in certain spots." She shows me the spots.

I'm hungry and want seconds, but don't want to give Karen the satisfaction that the food was that good. She changes the channel and watches the tail-end of the local news. They run a human-interest piece about a blind man who has learned to walk home from his job—they don't say what he does—without the use of his cane or seeing-eye dog.

"Did you see anything interesting today?" Karen says, wiping some sauce from her lips. "Did you finally get that fox?"

"No," I say.

"You'll get it."

Outside, night has finally settled in and the room is lit only by the pale glow of the television.

We get up some time later and Karen clicks on a few lights and I clear the dishes, sauce-covered napkins, and half-empty glasses of diluted iced tea. The TV's still going, playing some celebrity news.

"School all right?" I ask Karen when she comes into the kitchen.

"Mondays are always tough. Everyone's still got one foot in the weekend. Oh, here's today's mail." She hands me a thick stack. I sit down at the breakfast nook in the kitchen and begin to sift through the junk. There's another one—another bill from the hospital. They always look the same: a long rectangular letter with a little cellophane window in which my last name is misspelled. I push the mail aside and fetch the butter dish and serving platter from the living room.

The tight-faced anchor on the celebrity-news program can't stop yammering about Drake Rasmussen: "Did he really walk away from it all? And what does this mean for his upcoming movie *The Wine of Youth*?" The man's voice is piercing and all I want to do is locate the clicker and shut him off. I finally find it underneath the coffee table and line it up with the screen and go to press POWER.

And I stop.

It's him.

The man from the mansion.

His hair is longer and his skin is more tanned in the photo they show on television, but I'm certain it's him. "Who is this?" I ask.

Karen shuts off the running tap and pops out from the kitchen. "Oh, that's what's-his-name… the dreamy man all the girls are nuts for. Drake something. I read a piece on him in a magazine recently." Karen goes on and I stare at the different photos that pop up on the TV. "He's a bit of a wild thing… lots of trouble with alcohol… endless romances…"

I nod.

"Why?" she asks.

"Just curious," I say, listening to the anchor a little longer: "Why would he walk away from it all at thirty-one," the man says. "What is he doing now? Where is he?" They move on to the next segment and I shut off the television.

* * *

Karen gets ready for bed and I lean against my dresser and gaze out my bedroom window. The moon's light dapples the tranquil water while wisps of clouds work their way across the sky. I stare at a few puffs and wonder where they'll be in an hour.

Karen enters and rubs the top of my head. Her touch is warm and light as powder. She turns and takes to her room, calling out goodnight as she shuts her door.

In time, I, too, slide into my bed. Sleep doesn't come easy to me; closing my eyes just gives my brain more power, and I think of tumbling off the ladder: almost in slow-motion, over the metal, arcing through the air, and pounding on the asphalt. Just like that. While I was hanging Christmas lights, a gust blew and I lost my balance. I reached for the roofline but couldn't grip it. I didn't wake up for two months. And when I did, there was no damage to my body or brain. I just sat up like I'd been napping, and Karen and my brother, Larry, were chatting at the foot of my bed. Larry was eating green jello.

Karen placed her hand over her mouth and rushed over and kissed me. She started crying in bursts; then the doctors rushed in and asked me some questions, performed some routine tests, and said it—said *I*—was a miracle.

Larry stayed at the foot of my bed and clutched my ankle. He closed his eyes and his lips bent in a small smile.

The doctors kept me at the hospital for two more days and then let me go back to the island. Larry even paid for us to take a helicopter instead of the ferry. He wasn't himself, though. He was usually the quickest guy but seemed slow that day, like his brain had been dipped in syrup.

The helicopter whirred over San Pedro and the Pacific and Karen gripped my hand as we hovered across the steady sea. She cried like at our wedding. "I can't believe it," she kept saying.

Weeks passed. Everything was the same. The paper—if you can call a periodical that reaches a hundred people a paper—even wrote an article about me. The headline read, "Miracle Man."

About two months later, Karen sizzled cheap steaks in a pan and I looked over some old photos in the kitchen. "Sweetie," she said, mimicking the same customary tonality that I'd adored for so many years. "I need to tell you something."

"Yes," I said.

Her cheeks were red and her hair was frizzy.

"All I do is think about those days in the hospital," she said. "You, with the feeding tube in your mouth, and me, shaving your face each morning and talking to you. I thought that was it."

"I know," I said.

She wiped a tear from her eye. She'd been crying so much lately; at this point, I wasn't even sure where the drops were coming from.

"I thought you were going to die. I was scared and lonely. I didn't want to be alone. I—"

And I don't know why I said it, but I did; I just said it like it was a line I'd been rehearsing: "You slept with Larry, didn't you?"

She was still. My heartbeat quickened and I could hear nothing. Not the waves outside, not the steaks on the burner, only her words: "Sixty-four days," she said. "The doctors made me feel worse. And he was there every day with me, grieving. That was a long time for him to be away. He loves you so much. And he reminded me of you, you know? It's—"

"Just stop."

"Conrad..."

"Stop."

A few days later when Karen was at work, I was home alone like usual, and I called Larry at his grain factory a little outside of Lawrence, Kansas. That's right: Larry from Lawrence.

There was a lot of background noise: buzzes, beeps, and a constant grinding sound.

"Larry," I said.

"Hey!" he said. "How you feelin'? Called last week, but guess you were out on the boat or something."

"I know all about it," I said.

"What?"

"I know."

"What?"

I didn't know if he was playing stupid or if he really couldn't hear. A whirling noise had been added to the mix.

"Karen told me," I said.

"I don't—"

"She told me about the two of you. I won't tell Debra," I said.

There was a long pause.

"Conrad," he said. "Wait..."

I hung up, thinking how miserable a miracle could be.

And this is what I do each night. This is my lullaby. Has been for the last ten months.

The moon's glow is so bright that I get up and lower the blinds. A steady rain is now falling and every so often, droplets find the window, making the faintest knocking sounds. I wonder about Drake Rasmussen. Why is he sad? I can picture him standing in that window with a cigarette in his mouth, his eyes close to tears. Everyone's just a house, I think, just a pretty house with fresh paint and bouncing flowers, but inside, there's always a man standing in the window, crying.

* * *

The next morning when I wake up and trudge downstairs, the TV's playing in the living room. A bombastic blond is dishing out the L.A. traffic report while Karen is spooning coffee grains into the pot. She's in her usual blue robe, emblazoned with a dozen or so crescent moons. One of the moons on her back has a small tear in it, and through the hole I can see a bit of flesh.

"Good morning," she says.

"Morning. How'd you sleep?" I say.

"Fine." She places her hand on my shoulder. "Had a really strange dream, though. We were back in France… you remember that trip to Aix-en-Provence? Well, in the dream you kept ordering gin and it never came."

"I can't remember the last time I dreamt."

"We all dream. Some just can't remember."

I sit down at the breakfast nook and stare out the window. A thick marine layer surrounds the island like a protective shield and a vicious wind rushes over the house, almost purring as it rattles the roof. The mail's still there, in a heap, at the far end of the table. The hospital bill pokes out from the bottom. My insurance covered most of the costs, but I find myself having to pay about twenty-thousand dollars. Two months in the hospital is more expensive than renting a villa in Switzerland. We've worked it out so that we can pay a little at a time, but I'd love these bills to stop coming. It's a reminder of the fall, of Karen saying that she found me with a "crown of blood around my head," and of Larry eating his green jello.

Karen places a tray of toast, jam, and a pot of coffee on the table. She slinks into the nook, across from me. She talks about one of her students, a boy from Korea. The coffee awakens my brain and lifts my morning fog. While Karen gibbers, an idea forms, grows in my mind, and gains strength each time I glance at the large rectangular bill peeking out from the bottom of the pile: The anchor on TV said that Drake Rasmussen was retiring. I bet a picture of what he's currently doing would be worth some money. Maybe not twenty grand, but still—something.

* * *

After Karen leaves for school, I get ready: grab my assorted lenses, my binoculars, and even some fishing gear. I'll seem more discrete if I pretend to be fishing.

Outside, the wind thunders, providing for a brash sea, but nothing I can't handle. I leave the house, hop into my skiff, and motor off. The skirling of the wind is so strong that I only faintly hear the purr of the engine. No boats are out today.

I wonder what Drake is doing right now. I hope he hasn't left. It's certainly possible. I've never taken a photo for a celebrity-type magazine, but they pay more for humans than for nature; that's for sure. Paparazzi, they call them. Paparazzo, I think, if it's only one. When I worked for a car magazine a long time ago, this intern always spoke to me about how he used to spend his weekends outside posh L.A. restaurants, hoping to spot celebrities. One time, he snagged a couple photos of an actress's newborn and was paid something like thirty-two grand.

In the distance, I see the spray of whale spouts. Normally I'd set up camp, but today I zoom past them and press on. I'm only about ten minutes away now. My hands cramp up from the cold, and I bring them to my mouth and blow hot breath on them. Underneath the skiff is a tornado of sardines, swirling in flicks of quick light.

The mansion comes into focus and I loosen the throttle. The engine goes from hearty growl to gentle hum. When I get closer, I kill the motor and bob like a piece of driftwood. For now, it looks as though no one's home: the outdoor lights are off and the shades are drawn.

I'm glad I've planned on being a fake fisherman today. In time, I've set myself up pretty good. I cast a line. There's no bait at the end, which makes me the most honest fisherman in the sea. Maybe there's a lonely bass that's been trying to find a way out and will be happy to see my hook.

In time, the quiet gets to me, and it comes back in flashes: Karen's big, wet eyes, the fall, the slow-mo feeling, the doctor's mustache, and the green jello. I shake it off. Thirty-nine years is too much to just move on. I'm too old. She's too old. I've always liked that my generation wasn't a bunch of quitters. We were all about finding *the one;* these days, it's all about finding *someone.*

I pull out my binoculars and work them across the mansion. Nothing. Maybe he's sleeping, though. It was stupid of me to get here so early. He's a Hollywood guy. Why would he be up at eight-thirty in the morning?

The wind has subsided and the marine layer has lost some mass. By ten, I think, it should be clear. The Pacific isn't a morning person either. I set my binoculars on my lap and turn back to fishing: cast off, yank the rod, straighten my arms, and listen to the line hiss.

A rumble interrupts the tranquility, and soon after, there's a visual to accompany the noise: a yacht, going too fast, approaching the island, moving in towards the mansion. Could it be him? At this hour? Where has he been?

The yacht closes in. It's now no more than a couple-hundred feet away. Music, something with a high-pitched guitar, mixes with the salinity of the air. I bring my binoculars to my eyes and inspect the yacht's flying bridge. It's most certainly Drake. He hasn't got a shirt on, at this hour, in this cold, and sitting next to him is a man drinking from a large clear bottle. The man seems older with a sizable bald spot on his crown. He is also bare-chested and his left pectoral is tattooed with a rendering of the Virgin Mary. When the yacht gets closer, I drop my binoculars onto my lap and return to fishing. I even whistle. There's no way they can hear my whistle, especially with the growl of their engine, but the tune just says, "I'm alone. And I'm minding my business." That's the beauty of age. No one really expects anything from you.

The yacht rushes past me and Drake drops the engine into low gear; the motor makes a belching sound and the wake fans out and rocks my boat, causing my binoculars to fall from my lap into the hull. I leave them down there and stare without aid at the stern of the yacht. *Poseidon* is written in fancy letters across the back of the ship, and now, standing portside, is the other man. He's still clutching the bottle and we inspect one another and he doffs an imaginary hat. He even takes a small bow, and I laugh.

I turn away from Drake and the man, and face eastward. The wind has died down, and the ocean is calm again. There's nothing out here for miles. Just blue smoothness, just like the flatlands outside of Larry's Eastern Kansas; except instead of corn and rye, it's salt and sea, waves and foam.

After a few minutes, I turn back around. I don't want them to be suspicious, and my lack of attention towards Drake has probably helped solidify that I'm an old fisherman and that I know nothing of Hollywood. They probably think I'm a geezer who calls the movies "the show." I pluck my line from the sea and inspect the tip.

A voice skips across the water: "It's enough!" I hear.

I bring my gaze around and dip my line back into the ocean.

"You're such a fucking coward," the man yells, trudging back up to the home. Drake is still tying the yacht to the dock. He's silent. I want to take a picture but fear he'll spot me. I don't even reach for my binoculars. Drake pulls something from his pocket and then, moments later, pops a cigarette between his lips.

The current pushes me away from the mansion, and I want to power up to hold my ground, but fear that the sound of the motor will call attention. I reach for my camera, but Drake starts moving up the stairs and the boat is rocking and there's too much moisture in the air. I let the ocean play with my boat for a little longer and watch Drake storm up the stairs, enter the mansion, and shut the patio door behind him.

Karen's voice enters my undistracted mind: "And you've been perfect?" she says. "I know I messed up. Beyond that. But I thought you were dead. I cried every day for two months. Have you ever cried for me?"

"I wish I was dead."

"You are, practically."

"Why the hell did you tell me?"

"The same reason you told me all those years ago. It's hard to live a lie. I wanted it out there. I want you and me to be strong again."

"It's not the same. Mine was stupid, on assignment with a woman whose name I can't even remember. It wasn't your sister."

"Conrad, please. We weren't perfect before. We had trouble. It's convenient to put it all on me… isn't it?"

And sometimes I think she's right. It is convenient "to put it all on her." We started sleeping in separate beds a few years before my accident. I'd had a gallstone operation, and the doctor advised me to sleep in another bed until I healed. Karen made sure I heeded the advice, and made up the guest room, and I slept better, snored in peace, and never returned to her side. I guess when I got married I thought the goal was comfort, to get to a place of absolute ease where my pulse would stay steady, but I'm not so sure that's good. At that stage, the things that brought you together—smiles, laughter, and goodnight kisses—are first to evaporate. Maybe it's best to stay a teenager for as long as you can.

* * *

A couple hours pass. Drake and the man are probably sleeping now. It seems as though the two of them have been having quite a time, so I think it's time to pack up and head home. Pretending to be a fisherman is tough. Pretending to be *anything* is hard.

One last time, I line my binoculars up with the façade and trace the windows. I spot movement and the French doors swing open. It's Drake. He's holding a guitar and smoking another cigarette.

The current has brought me far away from the mansion. I'm sure that Drake can see my boat, but there's no way he can tell that I have binoculars glued to my eyes. He begins strumming the guitar and every so often, I think a note or two reaches me. I can't tell what song he's playing, but while inspecting his face, it appears he's singing along. His hands are clad with rings and he contorts his fingers in different positions on the neck of the guitar.

In time, the other man joins him on the balcony and I pluck my camera from my lap, turn it on, and zoom all the way in. I'm far, but I'm still able to pop off a few shots. The distance is a problem, and there's still a great deal of moisture in the air. I want to get closer. I need to get closer. But I know I can't. Not now. They'll probably get scared off. I hold them in the aperture and secure a few more shots of the two of them on the balcony. When Drake stops strumming, the other man brings the tips of his fingers to Drake's cheek and Drake pushes him away. I'm so surprised that I nearly forget to shoot, but regain my senses soon enough and press my index finger down—once, twice, three times. Again, Drake shoves the man, and the man loses his balance and tumbles to the deck. I click. The moments freeze and file into my camera. My body stiffens, and I can feel an artery on the side of my neck snap and expand, snap and expand. Drake rushes into the mansion and slams the door behind him. The other man gets up slowly and clutches his mouth.

I yank the engine cord and the propeller sings its familiar whine. I drop the camera into my jacket, zip up, and take off. Karen said Drake was a ladies' man, right? Nothing about him being with other men. I twist the throttle hard and wonder what the editors will say when they see my photos.

* * *

It's half past three, and I'm upstairs in my room. Should I tell Karen what I've done? I would've in the past, but since the accident, I just do my own thing. Some have his-and-her sinks and his-and-her towels. We have his-and-her lives.

Before downloading the pictures to the computer, I check them on the camera's display screen. They're worse than I thought. The excitement got to me and I didn't pay close enough attention to the shots. The moments are captured, but the subjects are too far, and specks of moisture obscure Drake and the man's faces. There's no way to tell it's him. I scan through all of the shots, and they're all the same—covered in dots, their bodies distant. I let out a strong breath and inspect again. I'm disappointed; my goddamn adrenaline must've been pumping. The lighting isn't bright enough either, and I wonder how much longer the two men will be there.

With little else to do and my desire to learn about Drake Rasmussen, I type his name in a search engine. A plethora of photos pop up, some of him with other actors and actresses I *do* recognize. On one site, I learn that his real name is John Henry Shepard and that he grew up in Kentucky. He was raised by his mother, a truck driver. He attended Juilliard for a few months before dropping out to model and perform off-Broadway productions. There's a laundry list of women he's supposedly dated, too.

What's it like to get your name changed? I wonder. Is it like plastic surgery for your psyche? Do you start to act more like the man you want to be than the man you are?

I continue to scan Drake's bio. There's no mention about him being with men. A few rumors, but nothing serious. No proof.

* * *

Karen roasts chicken in the oven while I cut up carrots and stalks of celery for the salad. The chopping sound is rhythmic and consistently interrupts my thoughts. Karen hums a little tune and checks the bird. "Lookin' nice," she says. "Do you need help with the cutting?" She rubs her hands on a dish towel and smiles. With the glow of the kitchen lighting on her and the heat of the oven flushing her face and neck, she's as pretty as the day I asked her out. I was living in New York and she was a secretary at a photography magazine. I went in for an interview—one that I knew was a longshot—and after, was "thanked for coming in." She must have sensed my disappointment. I even played it up a little, tried to conjure more sympathy. "The least you can do is have dinner with me now. After your magazine ruined my day." She laughed, smiled, and agreed. She had a pen tucked in her hair. A red pen. That night, we enjoyed French cuisine at a bistro down the street, where the food was difficult to pronounce and even harder to pay for.

Karen pulls the oven door open. The chicken is golden and crackling and a wave of garlic and rosemary finds its way to me. She sticks a thermometer in the bird. "About two minutes more… say, how is the brochure coming along?"

"All right."

"Did you get that fox?"

"Uh, yes," I say, "but it's horrible. Too many moisture spots."

"You just need to get closer."

"Yeah."

"I know you," she says. "You'll get it. You always do whatever you have to do."

I plop the carrots and celery into a bowl and Karen adds some lettuce and dressing. In no time, we're at our post, in front of the TV. The news plays and we take bites. My mind drifts. I think of Drake and the man in that large house. I wonder how the man's mouth is, and if Drake is sorry.

Nighttime might be better, with more of a contrast, yellow lights against a dark sky. I'll wait for Karen to doze off and head over about midnight.

After we savor the last bites of chicken and salad, we clear the dishes and straighten up. Karen tells me she's going to turn-in early, that she feels like she caught a bug from one of her students.

I sympathize and go out to fetch the mail. It's the usual crap. Nothing like the mail of an old man to bring a person back to earth: prescription-drug flyers, sit-down shower pamphlets, and motorized-wheelchair brochures. There's another letter from the hospital, too—this one informing me of their annual gala. The theme is *Casablanca*. Just what I want to attend—a party with a ballroom full of seniors dressed like Bogart, muttering, "Here's looking at you, kid," while they babble about their arthritis and swallow pills with tepid water.

* * *

In bed, my brain reels and my fingertips tingle. I stare at the ceiling and wait. I listen to the tug of the ebb. Surf explodes against the island. How much abuse has Catalina taken from the sea?

Waves are essentially the heartbeat of the earth—years and years and they've been there, every moment, over and again, breaking and receding. Fast, hard, soft, but always there.

I close my eyes and try to visualize the photos I'll get. The two men, bright in the window, fighting, hitting maybe. I imagine how good it will feel to send in the pictures, receive all that cash, and write the hospital a check with the note: *Here is your money. Paid in full. Please never contact me again. We'll always have Paris... -Conrad.* I envision myself licking a stamp, adhering it to the envelope's corner, dropping the bill in the mailbox, and bringing the flag up.

At about midnight, I slide out of bed and get dressed. I sling my camera over my shoulder and take to the hall. Karen's bedroom door is cracked and I peek through the opening. The nightlight fills the room with weak wattage and it looks as though she's sleeping well, with a steady flow of breath. Yellow rollers fill her hair, and she's still on her side of the bed after all this time.

I tiptoe and press on to the stairs. I take them slowly, both feet on each step till I reach the end; then I pass through the living room and out the front door. I lean into the wind and hear the screech it makes as it assaults my ears. Finally, I make it to the dock, step into the skiff, and head off. I'm now far from the coast, completely at the mercy of the inky sea, slogging through cold blackness.

* * *

When I finally near the western side of the island, it's almost one. Tonight, the waves are sharp as broken glass. I'm beat. The hull's been riding up the crests of waves and slamming down with a thud. My ears hear nothing but wind. On the California coast, different cities glitter: Redondo Beach, San Pedro, even Malibu. I want to cut the engine and use my oar to get closer to the mansion, but if I do, the sea will have its way with me, so instead, I accelerate towards the mansion, hoping the small inlet will provide protection against the mighty Pacific.

The mansion is dark. No action. A rock with people inside.

Again, the skiff drops down a wave and splats onto the sea. Spray rises in all directions and much of the water lands in the hull, where it sloshes around my boots, penetrates the thick leather, and gets to my feet. I'm shaking. My teeth chatter. I just want to dock the boat and rest. If they spot me, I'll say, "I'm old… I got stranded at sea and panicked."

I jerk the throttle all the way back, fight against the storm, go against the tide, and approach Drake's dock. Most of the space is taken by the yacht. I'm forced to tie-down to the back of the Poseidon. Drake has boat fenders big as chairs that bumper his yacht's shell, and they absorb the impact with squeals as the winter sea slams me into them.

I didn't expect to be standing on Drake's property. But here I am, on his dock, facing the mansion. I've never been this close, and it's so much more impressive here than it is from sea. In the distance, down the left side of the house, I think I spot some light spilling from a window. Karen's words from this past evening come to me: "You just need to get closer… I know you… you always do whatever you have to do."

I creep down the left side of the house, step over tangles of undergrowth and splintered branches and broken twigs. I think about turning back, even glance in the direction of the dock, but my boat is now as far as the lighted window in the distance. I've come all this way. I'll just see what's at the window. If nothing's there, I'll go home.

The wind no longer tears at me; the mansion provides protection, and I continue to slink, my fingertips drifting along the outer stone wall with each step. The window is now only a few feet away. It's a bay window with three pieces. One of the windows—the part closest to me—is slightly ajar. I place my ear to the opening. At first, I don't hear a thing, but when the wind drops for a moment, I hear a voice pipe up that I think is the man's. "Come on," he says. "It'll be fun." There's a loud laugh and clinking glasses. My chest burns and I want to take a deep breath but fear the noise it will create. Pressure builds in my shoulders and legs, and my body stiffens. I gnaw the inside of my cheek.

When I peer through the glass, my heartbeat accelerates,

keeping time like a second-hand, and I know that despite the wind-scourged night, my face must be red. To my left is a fireplace with dwindling flames; in the center is a large coffee table, and to my right, is a blue couch. On the sofa, sits my prey, Drake Rasmussen. I can only make out his profile, but it's him. The guitar is on the floor and eye glasses are fastened to the collar of his t-shirt. His face is flushed and his hair looks wet. Moments later, the friend joins him, wearing only pajama bottoms and carrying two glasses of what looks like whiskey. A bit of flesh plumps over the sides of his waistband. He sits down on the sofa, too, right next to Drake, obscuring my vision of the star. The man's lip is swollen and blood has caked around the wound. I turn away and exhale till it feels like my lungs are completely deflated. I take a few more breaths, but my heart rate stays high.

I crouch below the sill and turn on my camera. If I get this shot, it'll just be labeled as two friends sipping liquor. While I'll get something for that, I doubt it will be enough for the hospital bill. I wish they would fight again—but it's hard to repeat the past.

I wait.

My left hand cups the lens and my right forefinger pressures the shutter release. In all my years of photography, it's never been easier. There he is, in golden lighting, and I know he's not going anywhere. Not like the birds or fish or lizards I've spent years stalking. I bring the camera over the sill and take in the scene through the viewfinder of my camera.

"I'm sorry," I think Drake says, getting up from the couch and sitting opposite his friend on the coffee table. Perfect, it's like he can hear me. It's like I'm telepathically transmitting my instructions: Drake, get up, sit over there… yes, on the coffee table, and stare into your friend's eyes.

I snap.

Drake brings his hands to his friend's cheeks.

Snap.

The friend clutches Drake's hands.

Snap.

I position my head closer to the window and strain my ears: "It's just so hard for me, you know?" I hear Drake say. They lean towards each other. Their heads touch, their bodies form a mountain, and their lips meet close to the summit.

Snap.

They kiss more, eyes closed, their hands on each other's necks.

Snap.

Drake opens his eyes and holds his friend's face only inches from his. Each of them blinks. The eye contact is powerful and, for a second, I forget exactly why I'm here. The scene is not what I would describe as traditionally beautiful, but in all my shootings, I've never captured love. Sure, I've seen lions and their cubs and birds jumping from nests, but humans are the only animals capable of this. The friend lays his head on Drake's chest.

Snap.

Drake says something, but a gale rattles through and I lose his words. The wind falls and it's easier to hear him once again: "It's hard to drive so many miles without getting lost every now and then."

The friend nods and the two of them lean into one another and embrace. I'm a little slow on the trigger, and the friend's face lowers and obscures Drake's features.

"I love you," I think the friend says.

They pull away from one another for a second, as if to see if each other is real after those words are spoken. The friend blinks slowly and chews on his right thumbnail, while Drake's lips bend and a dimple surfaces on his right cheek. It's deep and a perfect crescent-moon shape.

Snap.

The friend lets go of Drake's hand, reaches for his glass of whiskey, and takes a good pull.

Snap.

Drake rises from the coffee table, returns to the couch, and plops down. A feather from one of the pillows shoots out and flutters like an autumn leaf behind them.

Snap.

The two of them nuzzle and mutter in voices too soft to reach the window.

Snap.

"I say we go for it. No one will expect us to come at this hour," Drake says. And he laughs. His laugh is raucous and such a divergence from the tenderness that I'm startled and nearly lose my footing.

"All right," the friend says, pushing off the couch. He trips over the coffee table, then staggers to a room on the far end of the house.

Snap.

Drake stays on the sofa, in front of the fire, now drinking from his friend's tumbler. His eyes are glassy and he seems tired. There's a small serpentine scar under his eye. Did he get it as a boy? As an adult? With this friend?

He plays with a strand of loose hair and then stares right out the window—the window I'm peeking into. I inspect him through the viewfinder. I'm at the bottom of the glass, near the sill, and unsure if I should budge. If I duck down, I'll disappear, but he may spot the movement. On the other hand, if I stay tucked away at the bottom of the window, motionless, I may just be giving him more time to spot me. I stay still. I'm too scared to do anything else. He looks relieved, though, maybe at peace. I'm not sure what peace looks like. I wonder how long he has been in love with this man. In time, he brings his gaze back to the fire, finishes off the last inch of whiskey, and runs his tongue along his teeth.

Snap.

Then he gets up and makes his way to the same bedroom as his friend and shuts the door behind him. It's just me and the living room, the tired fire, the squashed pillows, and the empty glasses. I think about staying longer. Maybe there will be more photos, but I check what I've got, and it's all clear and usable, without question Drake Rasmussen, and I'm cold, and for the first time in a while, tired.

I skulk away from the window. My legs are stiff and don't awaken easily. Once, then twice, I hear the exhausted fire pop, and the sound is frightening, like someone is shooting at me from behind. I pick up the pace; though I still peer down to make sure I don't trip. My camera swings from my neck like a pendulum and the itchy strap chafes my skin. In time, the whole process seems like a dream—the wind howls and it's now raining. The waves thunder below and shatter on the rocks. I should be on the dock soon, I tell myself. They're in the house. You're doing fine. You got the pictures. Karen is at home, sleeping a deep sleep. Big dreams. The dock is close.

When I finally reach the edge of the house, the wind has no obstacle and goes at me like an angry drunk, nearly pushing me into the brush. I crouch and make myself smaller, so that the wind will have less to attack. In this fashion, I manage to creep towards my boat. The sea flays the dock and water bursts and pelts my face. The moon's light is strong and because of it, I'm able to hop onto Drake's yacht safely. When I transfer from the Poseidon to my boat, though, my hand slips from the metal railing of the yacht and I lose my balance.

I plummet into the Pacific.

The sea is black and frigid. I kick my legs and squirm about the roaring water. My eyes prickle with salt, and because I'm heavily dressed, my body feels weighty and immobile. I thrash and wade through the darkness, claw towards the surface. When my head pops free, I gasp; I inhale so deeply that it triggers a violent cough. Another wave lashes the shore, tosses me in its mass, and I flounder, my arms splaying in all directions. I want to scream. I want to yell for help, but I'm deep underwater, in complete blackness. The only thing that tells me I'm alive is the stinging of my eyes and my body's need for air. Another wave belts the shore, and I'm forced to ride its current. The water's tug, however, has guided me into the rope that holds the Poseidon and my skiff together. I burn all the strength I have and yank myself onto my boat and tumble into the hull. Again, I cough. My shoulders twitch. Rain assails my face and drops of fresh water mix with salt water. I'm not sure how I was able to pull myself up, but I don't ask questions. A keen twinge stings my arms as I continue to frantically breathe. I know my photos are ruined, but somehow the camera has managed to stay around my neck. I sit up, chilled and scared; my hand quivers as I tug the motor's cord and a strong odor of gasoline floods the scene.

I'm off, over winter seas, towards my home on the southern

side of the island. Tears burn as they sprout from my eyes, and every now and then, my free hand wipes the droplets from my face. My fingers can't tell what is rain and what is not. When I'm halfway home, I remove the camera from my neck, hurl it into the sea, hear a heavy plunk, and imagine its mass sinking through black water.

* * *

I enter the living room. The couch's cushions wear our indentations from earlier in the evening and the lingering smell of garlic and rosemary still perfumes the home. Everything is just as it was when I left, and I'm both saddened and comforted by this: I'm still alive, but I'm back to square one.

Moonlight parts the blinds and illuminates the thick carpet like a hopscotch game, and I step softly into the boxes and make my way up the stairs.

I check on Karen, see that a quilt has fallen to the floor, and I enter her bedroom, scoop up the blanket, fan it out, and drape it over her legs. She exhales and I stare at her for a moment longer before taking to my room.

Once there, I peel off my soggy clothes and fling them into my bathtub. I run my hands over my bare arms, erase clusters of goosebumps with each stroke, and pull on my pajamas.

Still cold, I reach into my desk drawer and take a good pull of rum from a bottle. It's warm and reviving. Then I lumber down the hall to the thermostat and push the needle far to the right. I return to my room and get into bed. I listen to the sea. Pacific, I think, stands for peace, but it's anything but peaceful. I don't expect sleep to come quickly, especially with the eddying of so many thoughts, but it does. I shut my eyes and feel the drift.

* * *

Morning light pierces my window and rain strikes the glass. I'm quickly reminded of the night before when I get up and stagger to the bathroom with cramped muscles.

Downstairs, Karen cracks eggs into a pan bubbling with butter. The local news is on in the living room and the anchorman babbles about L.A. traffic. Of course it's bad—it's always bad. Why would today be any different?

Karen looks my way as I pull a mug from the cupboard and help myself to some coffee. "Were you cold last night?" she asks. "Got up this morning and found the heater up to eighty."

"Yes."

"You okay now?"

"Better. Did you sleep all right? You get rid of whatever you were coming down with?"

"Yeah, I think so."

We eat our eggs and I sop up the yolks with a piece of bread. The newsman's voice gets loud and the words "breaking news" are said multiple times. Karen pushes out her chair and steps into the living room. I take a sip of coffee, add some sugar, and stare out the window. My boat is there, tied to the dock, going with the way of the sea. The Pacific remains agitated with copious amounts of whitecaps dotting its body.

Near the dock, in a thicket of tall brush, I spot a dark mass. It moves, parts the long blades of brush, and comes into focus. It's the endemic Catalina fox. The luster of its gray coat sheens in the morning light, and its tail is bushy and coiled at the tip. I watch it until it decides to move on and scurry off, back into the brush.

"Oh, dear," Karen says. "Oh, dear."

"What is it?" I say, shuffling into the living room.

"You know… the guy we saw on TV the other night, the actor…" She scoots over on the couch and I slide in next to her. She points at the screen and I read the ticker that runs across the bottom: *Actor, Drake Rasmussen, 31, found dead off the coast of Malibu.* I feel my throat constrict and turn up the volume. The program brings in a reporter who tells the story: "Good morning," the woman says, "this is a fluid situation and we're learning more, but here's what we now know: Last night, Drake Rasmussen and a friend tried to battle stormy seas and took a yacht from Catalina Island to Malibu to attend a party. They were traveling at a high speed when they crashed into a rock. In the collision, they were thrown overboard. Drake Rasmussen was found this morning, close to shore, by a group of surfers, not far from his Malibu home. He was pronounced dead by authorities, drowning the probable cause." The program shows a photo of Drake being carried across the sand by paramedics in a body bag and I clench my fists and inhale a deep breath. "His friend, Neil Moren, survived the crash by clinging to a buoy for more than three hours. He was spotted by a local fisherman and is at an area hospital being treated for hypothermia." Photos from moments after the rescue are displayed. A heavy blanket is wrapped around Neil in one picture, and, in another, his head is buried in his hands while a woman rubs his back. Then they run photographs of Drake and Neil over the years—at premiers and restaurants, benefits and fundraisers. "Neil Moren," the anchor says, "has been described as Drake's manager, business partner, and closest friend."

I see the two of them, in the mansion, in front of the fire, kissing, holding hands, their lips wet with whiskey. I hear their voices and see the down feather fluttering behind the couch as they whisper sweet-nothings.

"Oh, my. They were here on the island," Karen says.

"He lost his best friend," I say.

"It's terrible," she says.

"I know," I say.

We turn our attention back to the TV, where the news now shows viewers an aerial shot of the wreckage. Scraps of metal and plastic are strewn about the Pacific, floating atop the foamy sea. They zoom in on the stern of the ship; the word *Poseidon* has been chopped in half and now reads *idon*. My hand trembles as it works its way along the couch cushions and finds Karen's fingers and grips them. I want to say, "I'm sorry." I want to say, "We can be better." I want to say, "Let's try and be like before." But I don't. Instead, I think of Drake and whisper, "It's hard to drive so many miles without getting lost every once in a while." Her body shudders and I hear soft cries. I shut my eyes and press tightly against her. "Conrad," she says. "Conrad." I draw in the spicy trace of her cinnamon soap, and we stay together, high in our home, all that water beating around us.

YOU'RE WITH ME

* * *

Tess stops outside the tattoo parlor on Raymond Avenue in Pasadena. She lingers by the front window, shifts her weight back and forth, and stares at the flowers, Chinese symbols, animals, skulls, and other bad ideas that plaster the walls. People sit on leather couches and scan binders; others yank up their t-shirts to show each other their fresh ink. Tess thinks about it, even pulls the door open just enough to hear the buzz of the needle.

* * *

After work one day, Tess entered a crowded bar and slinked into a booth with a couple other flight attendants. Not far from her, at a table off to her right, sat a sweet-looking man with thinning curly hair and a thick beard. He reminded her of her first boyfriend, unassuming and gentle. She threw him a glance every few minutes, but he didn't budge. His stare was straight, directed out the window in front of him. But once, when Tess turned her head, he rotated his, and their eyes held one another's for a few seconds. In her twenties, she wanted it all: handsome, funny, interesting, with a good job and healthy salary, but now, at thirty-six, she was fine with committed, honest, kind, with some hair.

* * *

She peels back the sleeve of her blouse and takes a peek at her forearm. Of course it's still there, she thinks, why wouldn't it be? It's a tattoo. That's its job. She traces her forefinger over each of the loopy letters.

* * *

He leaned against her table. He was taller than she expected, and had more of a presence, too. "Hi," he said. Tess noticed that a few of his fingernails were bruised. Her co-workers were quiet, but then realized they were too quiet and that their eavesdropping was obvious, so they resumed talking, but in hushed voices. "Listen," he said, "we're both attracted to each other, so rather than sit here and play these bullshit games and pretend we don't like each other when we really do... all I want to know is, do you have room in your life for a guy like me?" Tess pulled a sip of her daiquiri through her straw. "I don't know you," she said. He laughed. "That's true. I don't know you either." He ordered another beer. Tess's co-workers stayed a little longer, barely finished their drinks, then left. Tess shared stories about flying all over the world, unruly travelers, and how she always stopped one song short of a complete album because she didn't like the idea of fully finishing something. "What's your name?" she asked. "CJ," he said.

* * *

Tess enters the tattoo shop. She doesn't approach the counter to tell the receptionist—whose piercings must make it hard for her to pass through airport security—that she wants an appointment. She sits down next to a young woman who's holding a photo of ballet slippers, smiles politely, and feels her pulse thump.

* * *

In bed one night, Tess scanned a magazine and CJ's gaze rested on the whirling blades of the ceiling fan. "Did you find anything today?" she asked, folding down a page of *Redbook*. "I asked around and my friend can probably hire you part-time as a baggage handler if you want." She brushed her hair away from her face. CJ let a breath rattle from his lips. "You know," he said, "can I tell you something?" Tess nodded, and CJ continued: "I lied to you earlier. My parents are dead. They were killed in a house fire a few weeks before I met you. I never knew I was going to fall for you like I did, so I didn't tell you—I thought what's the point, you know? Since then, though, I've just felt like staying in, being quiet, being with you." Tess cried and ran her fingers over his chest and along his stomach. He told her that as soon as he felt a little better, he'd look for some construction work. Truly, though, Tess didn't mind that he was unemployed. When her dad had passed a few years ago, he'd left her 215,000 dollars, and she thought at this point in her life a man was far more important than anything else, and she believed—knew, actually—that her dad would agree. "Do you have any secrets from me?" CJ asked, placing his hands behind his head. His deodorant had caked onto some of his armpit hairs. "No," she said. "I just feel so bad for you. My parents were such a big part of my life. My mom still is. When my dad died, my mom always said that he was her happy ending."

* * *

Again, Tess glances at her tattoo. The letters *CJ* spill into one another like roots. The receptionist asks her if she's waiting for someone, and Tess answers no, that in fact, she'd like to speak with one of the artists and get a tattoo.

* * *

CJ watched basketball on TV, his face too close to the screen and his language rough. Eventually, his team pulled it out with a "hell of a shot, a prayer… sometimes it's better to be lucky than good," he said to Tess as they sat down for lunch. As he talked about the game he had just finished watching, he gestured, and petals from the peonies in the center of the table swayed to the varnished surface. "You okay?" CJ said. Tess's eyes grew big. "Yes, I'm fine," she said, pulling out a little white stick from her pocket. "Two lines… I'm pregnant!" she said. CJ pushed out his chair and clicked off the TV. "Wow!" he said. "Really? Are you sure?" Tess kissed CJ as spring wind rattled the screen doors around the house. "Yes," she said, "I'm sure. I took three of 'em."

* * *

A tree? A bird? Some flowers? Tess thinks. She doesn't know what she wants to do with CJ's letters. With the artists busy, she has time, and she even grabs one of the binders from the table in front of her and flips through the laminated sheets, hoping for some inspiration.

* * *

They went back and forth about the name, but decided on Emily. The name did something to CJ. When they brought their little girl home and placed her in the bassinet, Tess spotted CJ crying. "Sweetie," she said. CJ took Tess's hand and seemingly studied Emily's rosy face and tiny lips. "This feeling," he said, "I've just never had it before. Loving something so much almost makes me sad." That night, neither Tess nor CJ slept much as they constantly got up to admire their little girl. They stood there—in the dark room, the beat of crickets in the background, weak moonlight working its way through cracks in the shutters—overlooking their Emily.

* * *

Tess reapplies some lipstick and drags her tongue against her front teeth to make sure her smile won't be blotched. The tattoo artist—who introduces herself as Star—parts a blue curtain and invites Tess to the back. There, Tess shows Star her forearm and explains what she wants. Star brings out a pad of paper and begins to sketch.

* * *

For dinner, CJ served roasted chicken, creamed spinach, and some black rice. After most bites, Tess turned towards Emily to make sure she was okay. "When I head back to work in a few months," Tess said, "are you okay staying home and taking care of Em?" CJ nodded, his mouth full. Tess added some sugar to her iced tea, and CJ picked up a drumstick and ripped the meat from the bone. "You need to go to a doctor or something," she said. "All those nightmares aren't normal. I heard you last night, mumbling, sometimes screaming."

* * *

Star flattens out the piece of paper with the palm of her hand. She asks Tess if she likes it. Tess can't answer. Her throat tightens and she finds it difficult to swallow.

* * *

"I can't believe you did that!" CJ said, staring at his name inked on Tess's forearm. "Is it sore, or can I touch it?" he asked. Tess giggled. "Sure, you can touch it. I was walking by a shop and just decided to do it. You always hear about guys getting women's names on their arms. And I thought... hey, I can be a guy!" Their laughter was halted by a dog's bark near their front door. CJ got up and pulled the door open. "Hey, buddy," he said, rubbing a black Lab. "His name's..." CJ bent down and checked the dog's bone-shaped tag. "Feather." The dog barked and Tess shushed it because Emily was sleeping. CJ read Tess the phone number and she dialed. A man answered with a "Yeh-llow." Tess hadn't heard that greeting in some time, and she did her best to restrain her laughter. She let the man know that Feather was safe, and that they'd keep him at their place. "Oh, gracious," the man said. "Thank you, thank you... we'll be right over... you guys are right down the road, actually."

* * *

The artist leads Tess to a black, dentist-looking chair. Once there, Tess removes her blouse and gives Star her arm as though she's donating blood. Star shaves off some peach fuzz. She then cleans the area with alcohol. Tess strangely enjoys the tingle, the medicinal smell, and the quick evaporation.

* * *

A man and a woman trudged to the front door—he with a grey goatee and she with white hair curled atop her head. The man wore sunglasses and an Army cap and the woman a sweater with a dove brooch. The dog barked and darted towards the man as Tess opened the door. "Feather!" the man said, rubbing his dog's ears. He then introduced himself: "I'm Hatfield." The woman shot him a look, and he continued, "And this is my wife, Dora." CJ came to the door with the baby monitor clipped to his belt. Something of a sigh oozed from the speaker. "Oh, what a beautiful sound… wish I'd had one of those… would've saved me a lot of walking," Dora said. Tess laughed, then added, "I bought the best one on the market and I'm never more than twenty-feet away." Dora patted her dog: "Sorry about this… we just moved and Feather's confused." Hatfield removed his cap and rubbed his bald head. Tess answered, "Yes, we saw the truck. Welcome. Where'd you guys move from?" Hatfield cut Dora off: "Last stop was San Francisco." Dora spoke up: "Say… would you guys like to come over next week, next Saturday? We'll be ready to have company by then." Tess politely declined. "Please," Dora said, "it'd make us happy. We haven't got any friends out here. It's destiny. Feather could've gone anywhere." Dora smiled, a few of her gold molars sparkling. "Okay," Tess said. "Sure." Hatfield cleared his throat, removed his sunglasses, and stared at CJ.

* * *

Once the spot is clean, Star adheres the stencil to Tess's pale skin, and Tess eyes a smattering of photos on the wall—pictures of proud people with their new tattoos.

* * *

CJ hummed "This Little Light of Mine" as he cradled Emily. In the bathroom, Tess turned on the tub's spigot. She cupped a handful of water and splashed it against her calf, then soaped up her skin and reached for her razor. When Tess got into bed, CJ had already fallen asleep. While she flipped through *Sunset,* she heard him muttering and noticed dew-like beads on his brow. "I'm sorry," he said. His voice then sharpened, and he woke up, shaking, gasping for breath. The baby still slept soundly. "You're fine… you're with me," Tess said, running her hand along his neck. "You're with me."

* * *

Star opens a new needle in front of Tess, careful to show her. After the needle is popped into place, Star clicks on the machine. Tess braces for pain.

* * *

"I feel like getting dressed up tonight," Tess said. CJ shook his head. "Tonight? For Hatfield and what's her name?" he said. Tess shrugged, then added, "What can I say? I've lost most of the baby weight, back around a size six, so I feel like looking good. But you have to also… otherwise I'll look nuts." Tess put on her best I-know-you-love-me face, and CJ dropped his arms to his sides. She slithered into a blue dress and he worked the zipper up. "You know what I want to do more than anything else," he said. "When Em gets older, I want to go to somewhere with a big lake where we can rent a canoe, just the three of us, and paddle. Dip the oars in and out of the water. Feel the air on our bodies. Maybe fish, eat what we catch. Just us and the wild."

* * *

Tess grimaces as the needle follows the lines of the stencil. She thinks that in a strange way the pain feels good, almost cleansing. She closes her eyes and tries to figure out where Star is in the drawing, if she can make out what is being inked.

* * *

They arrived at Hatfield and Dora's. The blue house was small, wrapped with an unkempt fence coated with morning glory. "I love you in that blazer," Tess whispered to CJ as they neared the front door. All the windows were open and classical music sprinkled the air like dust. "Wow, do you guys look nice, or do you guys look nice?" Hatfield said, letting them in, restraining an exuberant Feather. Dora greeted them as well. "And look at this little sweetie... what's her name?" Dora asked. "Emily," Tess said, lifting the baby carrier up so Dora could better see her. Hatfield motioned for them to come in, grabbed a bottle of champagne from the kitchen table, and began to peel off the foil and unscrew the wire cage. Tess asked Dora if there was a place where she could put Emily, as it was her bedtime. "In our room," Dora said, pointing the way. Tess did as she was told, set the baby down in Dora and Hatfield's bedroom, returned to the foyer, and handed the baby monitor to CJ. He turned the volume low and placed the monitor in his blazer pocket. Hatfield took a good gulp of champagne and smiled at Tess and ran his eyes over CJ's face. "Noticed you two were looking at these photos," Hatfield said. "This is me in Korea, and this one's me in Nam. Was a Staff Sergeant by then." Tess noted that CJ's hands were clasped together.

* * *

Star tells Tess she's impressed with her pain tolerance and that most people squirm whenever she adds white highlights. Tess glances at her arm, but it's hard to see exactly what's happening. Blood seeps from her skin and saturates a paper towel Star holds over the area. The blood forms a shape that Tess thinks looks like the U.S., albeit without Maine's mass jutting out into the Atlantic.

* * *

"You're going to have to give me the recipe," Tess said. "These pigs in the blanket are amazing." CJ smiled and dragged one through some mustard. Tess was proud he wasn't having trouble going out and being with people, especially older ones that she feared may have reminded him of his parents. "Is that you, Hatfield?" CJ asked, pointing to a photo on the wall of a man in uniform. "No, that's my son… he was gunned down two years ago in Afghanistan. CJ nodded, offered his condolences, and went to check on the baby. Feather barked at something or nothing in the distance. The classical music CD—Hatfield had said it was Bach—played its last notes and stopped spinning.

* * *

The needle zigzags across her skin, and Tess guesses that Star is shading. It feels like Star has swapped her needle for a scalpel, and Tess brings her head back and lines her gaze with the ceiling. On it, written in Gothic lettering, are the words NO PAIN, NO GAIN.

* * *

Dora served apple pie with ice cream and expensive brandy, a V.S.O.P., in little tulip-shaped glasses. "These crickets," Dora said, "are they as bad at your place?" Tess laughed. Hatfield poured a little more brandy in CJ's glass. "It's good, right?" Hatfield said. CJ nodded. "Yes, I've always been a Red Label guy, but this is tasty." As they continued to drink and talk in the soft lighting of the dining room, Tess noticed the way Hatfield inspected CJ, maintaining heavy eye contact and nodding softly between pauses as if encouraging him to speak. "What kind of work do you do?" Hatfield asked CJ. "Many different things—I worked as a janitor, at a marina, as a landscaper, even a roofer." Tess, a little chilly, asked for CJ's blazer and he gave it to her, exposing large perspiration stains under his arms. CJ shook out his napkin and dabbed his neck. "So you like being alone, huh? Are you working now?" Hatfield asked, finishing off the last drop of brandy in his glass. "No," CJ said. "Were you born here in California?" Hatfield asked. "No, down South," CJ said, sweat congealing on his forehead. "Oh. We lived in Florida for a couple years. When you get to be our age, Florida residency is practically a legal statute."

Hatfield headed over to the CD player. Feather followed, his tail thumping along the wall. "What kind of music do you like, CJ?" Hatfield asked. "Anything's fine, really," CJ said. Tess helped herself to another slice of apple pie. "Santana," she said, "or Muddy Waters. He loves those guys." Hatfield turned CJ's way, rubbed his hands together, and perused his collection. "Only thing close that I have—and it's not that close—is The Grateful Dead. Will that work?" he asked, winking.

* * *

Star takes a break, gets up, and gives Tess a bottle of water. Tess sips, sits, and thinks. She resists stealing a glance at her arm. She wonders how long it'll take to heal. She wonders when Emily will ask her about the story behind it, and she wonders what she'll say.

* * *

"Well, thank you, Dora. Thank you, Hatfield," Tess said. CJ fetched Emily from Dora and Hatfield's bedroom and returned to the front door with the carrier where everyone was saying their good-byes. "Lovely to *really* meet you both," Dora said. Hatfield stood, silent, his face ruddy and shiny. CJ gripped Tess's hand. "Don't forget the recipe," Tess said. There was a little more commotion and the last laughs and lines of a Saturday get-together before Tess and CJ stepped down from the porch and headed home. Twice, CJ turned and glanced back at the front door. The air was soft and hot and the crickets hushed as the couples' footsteps neared. Behind them, through open windows, Tess heard Dora and Hatfield clearing the table: dishes being stacked atop one another, forks and knives clanging, and rims of fine crystal dinging together like high-pitched bells. "What a nice night," Tess said, partly because she'd had a good time, partly because if Dora and Hatfield could somehow hear her, they'd be happy to learn they'd been fine hosts. CJ squeezed Tess's hand and locked fingers with her. Even though it was warm and she'd had a lot to drink, her hands were cold, and she loved that CJ's touch was always hot, tonight clammy.

* * *

Star asks how Tess came up with the idea, and Tess doesn't *really* answer; she says that it came to her while walking around, just popped into her head.

* * *

As CJ and Tess got ready for bed, words escaped from the baby monitor. Tess, who was hanging up CJ's blazer, yanked it from the inside pocket and turned up the volume. "Oh, look," she said. "I guess we forgot the other monitor at Dora's." She walked into the bathroom where CJ was brushing his teeth and set the receiver on the sink. "Listen," she said. Voices quavered from the speaker. "The fixed eyes, the focus," Hatfield's voice said, "and the tight lips... try to picture him without the beard. You see?" Outside, a gust powered through the trees, scattering leaves, and scraping the sides of the house. "It's all I could think about," the voice said. CJ rinsed out his mouth and spit; he slid his toothbrush into the holder. His fingers quivered as he clenched the towel rack.

* * *

Eighty-three days ago, Tess thinks, feeling the sting of the needle. Star tells her that it's almost there, to count to a hundred, maybe two hundred, and it'll be done.

* * *

Hatfield's voice continued: "Every time I looked at him, I saw it. I felt so helpless, though. Did you get the sense that he was—" The voice grew faint and the receiver went silent. CJ picked up the monitor and twisted the volume knob, clicked the device on and off, placed his ear to the speaker. Nothing. CJ set it back on the edge of the sink and didn't say a word. He swallowed hard. His breaths were stuttered and he clasped his stomach with his right hand. "He knows," he whispered. "He knows." Tess took a seat on the rim of the bathtub. "What are you talking about?" she asked. CJ joined her on the edge of the tub and shut his eyes.

***

Star sets the needle down and runs a rag across Tess's crimson forearm. Tess can't bring herself to look right away, but she eventually does. It's all there, perfect, looking better than the sketch.

***

CJ came clean, told Tess everything, all the things he'd kept to himself for the last four years, confessed that he'd driven home drunk one night on a two-lane road, Peach Orchard Lane, outside of Atlanta, and hit a young woman who was changing her tire. "She was standing there. I saw her. I saw her too late." He let Tess know his real name was Buck, and how he'd slammed the woman, and how he'd heard her, and how he could *still* hear her. "She crashed against the glass, shattered the windshield, then plopped behind the car, and I left, just bolted. Heard the beep of my car door grow softer and softer." He admitted to Tess that he didn't stop because he thought people were chasing him, and that he kept seeing the woman's face and bright green sweater in his mind. "Amelia Forrester. I remember reading about her in the paper the following day, seeing her on the news. Seeing my car and face on the news, too. It was all over the South. I got out of there, took a bus. I still think about Amelia and her mom. He knows my face. Hatfield knows who I am," he said, scratching his forehead hard enough to leave red wisps on his brow.

***

Tess inspects the tattoo and even brings the tips of her fingers to her tender skin: the water's there, tranquil and soft, pierced only by two drifting oars. The canoe bobs atop its glassy surface, and two people, two women—a mom and a daughter—fish out of one end, their short lines cast in the same area. In the boat's hull, CJ's name is completely concealed, permanently camouflaged by heavy lines and severe shading.

* * *

"I wanted to tell you, but I knew you were the kind of person that wouldn't want to be with me if I did," he said. Tess couldn't speak. She stared at her bare feet on the cold tiles of the bathroom floor. She was too sad to be angry. He walked into the bedroom, pulled a duffel bag from the closet, and stuffed it with clothes. "What about Emily? What about me?" Tess asked. Again, he swallowed hard. "I can't be here when he figures it out. You and Em love CJ, not Buck." Tess sat on the corner of their bed; her face was scarlet and her eyes burned. "I thought you were going to be my happy ending," she said. He shook his head: "I don't think there's such a thing, Tess. There are happy moments, but the end is always lonely—lots of quiet, a hospital bed, a few flowers." They argued over him staying, but he said he didn't want to go to jail at any cost—even if it meant never seeing her or his baby again. He pulled Emily from the bassinet. She was awake and her small, marble eyes played on his face. He drew in her scent, ran his thick hand across the fuzz of her head, and kissed her on her temple. He then approached Tess, but she turned away. "I always thought karma might take the back roads," he said, "that this day might come. I'll leave the car at the train station." Tess listened as his footsteps softened, as the screen door squeaked, and as the engine rumbled.

* * *

She asks Star where exactly *CJ* used to be, and Star points to a puffy patch in the center of the canoe, along the water line. Then

Star gives a routine speech about lotion, scabbing, and letting the skin heal. Tess stares at the tattoo for a few more seconds before Star wraps it with gauze.

* * *

That night, she lay on the couch with Emily and stared out at the quiet Santa Clarita hills. A couple times, she awakened in a panic after dozing off for a bit, certain that she could hear him, smell him, and feel him. One time, she even called out hello. Goosebumps sprouted on her forearms as bits of clarity flitted across her mind and she connected some of the scraps: In the year or so that they were together, he never looked for a job, always avoided large crowds, insisted on having her mother visit them, and stressed the fact that he "didn't like his business out there." But then again, she thought, he was the only man who made her feel like the woman she thought she could be. All of her surroundings seemed dipped in his essence: the kind caress of wind, Emily's soft sighs, and the sweet scent of posy in the backyard. Everything was the same, but wasn't.

* * *

Tess gets up from the chair; the throbbing is steady, but she knows it'll soon pass. She gives Star a hug and thanks her. Tess can tell from the look in Star's eyes that she wants to know the story behind the covering of *CJ*, but Tess doesn't say a word. She hugs her again, pays up front, and exits the parlor.

* * *

The next morning, Tess didn't move. She sat on her couch where she'd spent the night, cradling Emily and listening to the ebb and flow of her girl's warm breath. Light spilled across the carpet and the gossamer drapes swelled with even the smallest wind. At any moment, she expected to hear the clunk of his footsteps on the stoop. She wanted to hear the jingle of his keys and the groan of the old hinge, the one she'd been asking him to fix for months. And then, minutes later, as if a prayer had been answered, she did. Before he even had the chance to knock, she set Emily down, rushed to the door, and flung it open. It was Hatfield. He seemed in his normal, jocular mood. "Salutations," he said. "Haven't used that word in a while. It always reminds me of *Charlotte's Web*. That's a pretty gruesome book, though. Hope you wait awhile before reading it to Emily. That first line… you remember it… I think it's 'Where's Papa going with that ax?' Pretty nutty thing, right?" He talked more. Tess didn't make eye contact, instead staring past his head at the distant hills, clad with dry grass and cacti. "I'm here to give this to you," he said, handing her the monitor. She nodded. Then he asked if CJ was around. Tess shook her head. "He's out," was all she could muster. "Oh, okay," Hatfield said. "It just did me a lot of good spending time with him is all. Dora said I shouldn't say anything, but he reminds me so much of my son. It'll be two years next month since he passed, but it's still hard. Maybe I want to see it—who knows?" Tess started to talk, but her voice was delicate with a sound like it might break if somehow it could be touched. He kept on: "Thought about saying it last night, but didn't want to get emotional. Anyhow, we need to get together again soon." Hatfield said good-bye and waved in Emily's direction. He tipped the bill of his Army cap and walked the brick path to the street. A twinge shot through Tess's spine as she brought the door softly to its jamb.

* * *

Tess strolls the boulevard. The usual vision doesn't come to her—him, heading east, north, or south on a dusty open road. She doesn't picture his left arm dangling from the front window, air gliding through his fingers, over his wrist, and around his forearm. No, instead—with an hour to go before she has to pick up Emily at her mom's—she cruises the sunlit streets, ignores the broken conversations from passersby, and savors the sight of her bandaged arm in the reflection of store windows.

CPSIA information can be obtained at www.ICGtesting.com
Printed in the USA
LVOW10*0640260315

431968LV00003B/38/P